W9-DCF-204

PROPER INTENTIONS

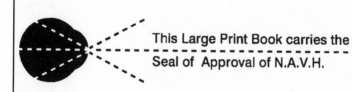

This Large Print Book carries the
Seal of Approval of N.A.V.H.

OHIO: BOOK ONE

Proper Intentions

THE YOUNG BUCKEYE STATE BLOSSOMS WITH LOVE AND ADVENTURE IN THIS COMPLETE NOVEL

Dianne Christner

THORNDIKE PRESS

An imprint of Thomson Gale, a part of The Thomson Corporation

THOMSON
GALE

Detroit • New York • San Francisco • New Haven, Conn. • Waterville, Maine • London

THOMSON

GALE

Copyright © 1994 by Dianne Christner.

All Scripture quotations are taken from the King James Version of the Bible.

Thomson Gale is part of The Thomson Corporation.

Thomson and Star Logo and Thorndike are trademarks and Gale is a registered trademark used herein under license.

ALL RIGHTS RESERVED

Thorndike Press® Large Print Christian Historical Fiction.

The text of this Large Print edition is unabridged.

Other aspects of the book may vary from the original edition.

Set in 16 pt. Plantin.

LIBRARY OF CONGRESS CATALOGING-IN-PUBLICATION DATA

Christner, Dianne L., 1951–
    Proper intentions : the young Buckeye State blossoms with love and adventure in this complete novel / by Dianne Christner.
      p. cm. — (Ohio ; book one) (Thorndike Press large print christian historical fiction)
    ISBN-13: 978-0-7862-9294-3 (lg. print : alk. paper)
    ISBN-10: 0-7862-9294-6 (lg. print : alk. paper)
    1. Ohio — Fiction. 2. Christian fiction, American. I. Title.
PS3603.H76P76 2007
813'.54—dc22
                                         2006035381

Published in 2007 by arrangement with Barbour Publishing, Inc.

Printed in the United States of America on permanent paper
10 9 8 7 6 5 4 3 2 1

Dedicated with devotion to my husband, Jim, whose love inspires me, and in memory of my grandmother Mattie.

CHAPTER 1

"Yoo-hoo, Kate!" The familiar voice grated on Kate's nerves like squeaky chalk. Melanie Whitfield stood across Beaver Creek's main thoroughfare waving her arms. Kate regarded Melanie as a meddler and gossip-monger. However, she was inclined to be kind toward all folks, so she started across the street.

The roadway was uneven and marred with ruts and rocks. Her foot slipped into a pothole, and the ladylike Miss Carson transformed straightway into a reeling drunkard. The next few seconds seemed like an eternity.

The earth tilted. The toe of her boot caught the hem of her long calico dress. *I can't fall in front of Melanie and the whole town,* she thought as she toppled forward with arms flailing.

Sprawled headfirst in the dirt road, Kate felt the sting of tiny pebbles embedded in her palms and a burning sensation in her knees. Grit caked her teeth, and her nose ached. She lay unbelieving and dazed until she heard Melanie's scream. "Look out, Kate!"

In a feeble attempt to shield herself from a thundering team of horses, Kate closed her eyes and threw up her arms. The driver of the rig strained to turn his animals. Jaws clenched, he braced his feet against the floorboards of the wagon. His heart did cartwheels when he spotted a young man charging toward the frightened woman. He breathed a prayer for them and yanked back on the reins.

Kate's rescuer plucked her from the ground and dove to safety as the huge beasts lunged past. When the dust cleared, Kate blinked and looked into a pair of familiar blue eyes that mirrored her own fright.

"Tanner!" she sputtered through a mouthful of grit.

"Are you hurt?"

Kate wiggled her ankle, which felt fine, and brushed off her hands and gown. "No, I don't think so."

Tanner supported her as she tested wobbly legs. "What a scare!" he groaned. Then he pulled her close.

Meanwhile, the driver of the wagon pulled his team to a standstill. Pitching the reins to his companion, he leaped to the ground and shouted, "Are you all right, Ma'am?"

Folks nearby stopped what they were doing when they heard the racket. A trapper in buckskin breeches turned to see what was causing all the commotion. Kate felt their curious stares and jerked away from Tanner's embrace. She raised a trembling hand and brushed at the black ringlets that clung tenaciously to her forehead. "Yes, just a bit shaken."

Melanie flung herself into Kate's arms and wailed, "I thought you were doomed." Then she folded her hanky and dabbed at Kate's dirt-smeared face.

The driver of the wagon spoke. "My apologies for the scare, Ma'am. I'm sure glad you're all right. The potholes in this road are big enough to swallow man, woman, or beast."

Kate felt concern in his scolding. She studied the young man with the ruddy complexion. "I don't believe we've met."

"Just moved to the valley, Ma'am. My name is Ben — Ben Wheeler."

"Pleased to meet you. I'm Kate Carson. This is Melanie Whitfield and Tanner Matthews."

Melanie hastened to greet the newcomer. "Welcome to Beaver Creek, Mr. Wheeler." Freckles spotted his face, and sky blue eyes gazed out beneath brown bangs and a droopy hat.

Wheeler warmed under the enthusiasm of the blond, frizzy-haired girl, but he quickly focused on Tanner who offered his hand. Ben gripped it tightly.

"Oh, and that's my brother Luke in the wagon." The siblings had similar features. The obvious difference was Luke's straw-colored hair. "I'd better be getting back to my rig. My apologies again, Miss Carson. I'm sorry about your dress."

Kate looked down at the tattered hem of her blue calico. "It can be fixed." She managed a smile in Ben's behalf. "Please don't give it another thought."

Ben gave his floppy hat a tug. "It was nice meeting you folks."

"We'll be seeing you around, Mr. Wheeler," Melanie called.

Tanner quickly took charge. "Let's get you ladies out of the middle of the road." They crossed the street. "Where are you headed?"

"Cooper's General Store to pick up the mail." Embarrassed from the incident, Kate stole a glance at Tanner and marveled that such a dashing young man was courting her.

He was tall, lean, and blond. His eyes were blue and penetrating, his smile dimpled.

At the General Store Tanner turned toward Kate, studying the petite creature that disarmed him so.

Kate's china-doll appearance often misled those who did not know her. She was neither fragile nor weak, but steady and strong in character. Tanner knew her strength stemmed from a faith in God. His gaze rested on the angelic face with its creamy complexion and soft brown eyes. Silky black tresses curled about her face, cascading far past her shoulders. Her lips were two delicate rose petals. He knew they were pure and untouched. Kate was very proper, and today was the first time she had been in his arms.

Kate shifted under his intense scrutiny. Often she felt uneasy around Tanner and did not know why.

Tanner grinned. "Take care, Darlin'. No more stepping in front of wagons. See you Friday night?"

Kate nodded. "Thank you, Tanner."

"At your service, Milady."

The instant he was out of hearing, Melanie whirled to face Kate. "Well! He's a Prince Charming, isn't he?"

"Tanner?" Kate hesitated. "Perhaps."

11

"Too obliging if you ask me, and bold as brass calling you darlin' in broad daylight."

"That's just the way Tanner talks. It doesn't mean anything. I saw the way you looked at that new fellow."

Melanie replied, "You certainly were clever, throwing yourself in front of his wagon. Let's see. Ben Wheeler." She rolled the words around on her tongue. "Yes, I do like the sound of that. Did you see his brother?"

"I did not throw myself in front of that wagon!"

"Ah-hum. Can I help ya, ladies?" Mr. Cooper interrupted. Propping his broom against the wall, he wiped his hands on his apron and waited on the girls.

"Oh, yes. We're here for the mail. How are you today, Mr. Cooper?"

Elias Cooper mopped the brow of his high forehead. A shiny bald head shone through brown hair combed straight back and styled long at the neck. His beard bobbed up and down when he spoke. "Fine, fine."

They followed him into the store, and he continued, "Over here. I'll git it for ya. It jest came in yesterday. Here ya are. Two letters for Miss Whitfield, and one for Mattie Tucker, which I'll be givin' you, Miss Carson. That reminds me, I've got some seed packets and a large parcel filled with items that Mattie wanted."

The girls parted, and Kate headed home, shifting the large parcel from arm to arm. She clutched the letter and seed packets. *Mattie will be tickled to see these,* she thought. Mattie Tucker had been a mother to her for many years — ever since the Indian raid that orphaned Kate and her two sisters, Annabelle and Claire.

The thoughts of the eighteen-year-old girl wandered here and there and finally settled on Melanie. *I didn't find out what Melanie wanted. Just as well, I suppose.* Then she remembered Melanie's warning about Tanner. She sighed. *Prince Charming is calling on Friday.*

CHAPTER 2

Kate thumbed through her Bible. The fragile pages fanned through her fingers and then lay open in the thirty-first chapter of Proverbs, where the words jumped off the page at her. "Favour is deceitful, and beauty is vain: but a woman that feareth the LORD, she shall be praised." She reread it, trying to take in the meaning.

Weeks at a time she would ponder over a single verse, for Beaver Creek had no church or parson to question. There was not a soul at Tucker House with whom Kate could discuss the Bible. Mattie was not a believer, but Kate's parents had introduced her to the Lord when she was a small child. Her faith was a link to her past that she adhered to with strong sentiments.

Kate mulled over the verse. *What does it mean to fear the Lord?* she wondered. *This verse is addressed to women. Don't men struggle with vanity? Especially capable men, handsome men . . . Tanner! Why he'll be here in less than an hour!* She reverently placed her feather bookmark in the page and fled to get ready.

Tanner Matthews's cattle ranch was a small jaunt away — five miles south of Beaver Creek. He entered the town riding his black stallion, Pistol. Tucker House, his destination, perched on the northern fringe of the settlement. On impulse, he reined in his horse at Green's Mill where Jake Hamilton worked. It was quitting time, and Tanner scanned the premises, hoping to have a word with Jake.

A drifter from Kentucky, Hamilton had hired on temporarily at the Matthews's spread two years earlier. Tanner had admired his reckless, worldly wise manner, and they became fast friends.

"You look scrubbed to a shine," Jake said in his lazy Southern drawl.

"On my way to Kate's."

"When you gonna figure out you're jest wastin' your time?"

"What makes you think that, Jake?"

"She's not your type. What about the gals in Dayton?"

"Don't worry, Jake. I'll still be making

trips to Dayton with you."

"I think you ought to jest forget her."

"Can't do that, Jake." Tanner reached out to steady Pistol, patting the beast's quivering neck. "It's too late. She's sweet on me. I got her melting like butter on a summer's day."

Jake shook his head and smirked. "Sure, Tanner. Maybe you can tell me about it later. There's gonna be a game tonight. Are you in?"

"I'll be there."

"Leave ya to your dreamin' then." Jake turned to walk away.

"Yeah, so long." Tanner spurred his horse into motion. His mouth curled up in a lopsided grin. No girl was unattainable.

Kate's sisters were sitting on the front porch steps when Tanner arrived at Tucker House. Annabelle was a mixture of mischief and delight, having a neverending source of energy. At thirteen, she teetered between womanhood and childhood. Her chestnut tresses bobbed up and down with wisps of cinnamon fluff framing her face. Claire was the baby of the family, which made her seem even younger than her tender twelve years. Atop golden plaited hair, her bonnet was askew, bouncing on her shoulders with ribbons streaming through the air like a kite tail.

"Evening," Annabelle said sweetly. "He's sure a beautiful horse."

"Got him for my sixteenth birthday."

"Can we pet him?"

"Sure. Look here, fella. Two pretty ladies want to meet you."

Pistol nodded his head as if he agreed, and the girls giggled.

Claire's blue eyes danced as she quipped, "Are you here to see Kate again?"

"As a matter of fact, I am." He winked. "Is she home?"

Mattie was just coming out of the kitchen when they entered the sitting room. She smoothed back her hair. "Mr. Matthews, good to see ya. Won't ya have a seat? I'm sure Kate will be down in a minute."

"Thank you, Miss Tucker."

Tanner had a few minutes to wait until Kate appeared followed close at the skirts by Claire. "Hello, Tanner." She seated herself in a wooden rocker.

"You shouldn't keep a fellow waiting, Kate, with Tucker House packed full of lovely ladies."

"This is too soppy! Come on, Annabelle." Claire left the room, leading her sister by the arm.

Mattie laughed and busied her hands, hemming a gown. "It's a lovely evenin'," she said.

"It is. Would you mind if I took Kate for a walk, Miss Tucker?"

"Of course not. Enjoy yourselves."

Once they were outside, he directed Kate around the back of the house toward the creek. It was a lovely spot, thick with springtime growth. Wild lilac bushes lined the path, and small trees congregated in clumps along the creek bank. Crickets chirped in harmony with hoarse frogs. Occasionally a hungry trout flipped out of the water, producing elaborate rings of silver that drifted away with the current.

"Are you fully recovered? Any scrapes or bruises?"

Kate answered pertly, "I think it is very rude of you to bring up such an embarrassing incident." She smiled. "I feel fine — except for my pride."

They watched the sun set from a hill that overlooked the countryside. When it slipped behind the trees, Tanner led Kate to a crude bench beneath the hickory tree that spread its limbs wide over the house. "Sit here awhile and watch the moon come out?" he asked.

Kate nodded. As the first shade of night

fell, the air turned cool. Kate shivered, and Tanner moved closer. "Cold?"

"I'm fine. The night is lovely, but the sounds are eerie."

"Animals. They just killed a big panther at the mill this week. You're not scared, are you? I'm handy with this, you know." Tanner patted his pistol, which hung strapped to his hip. He continued, "I've scared off plenty of wild beasts. I was in a gunfight once in Dayton."

"A gunfight! How awful. What happened?"

Tanner hesitated a moment as he mentally pieced his story together, summing up the parts he would leave out. "Not so terrible. I caught a man cheating in cards. He went for his gun, and I shot him in the arm."

"I've heard those kinds of things happen often when men gamble."

"You don't approve?"

"Does any woman?"

Tanner thought about the painted Stella at the Six Star Saloon in Dayton. She approved of anything he did. He grinned sheepishly and lied, "I guess not, Kate. Then there was the time we caught Indians stealing our cattle."

Kate stiffened. "Indians killed my folks, you know."

"No, I didn't."

Kate shuddered. She still had vivid dreams about it. Tanner seized the opportunity and drew her closer, slipping his arm around her.

"I was only six. Annabelle was one and Claire just a baby. We lived at Big Bottom on the Ohio River. Father hid us in the root cellar, but I could hear the shots, the screams — and smell the smoke. It was awful."

"Oh, poor darlin'." In a practiced motion, he tilted her chin and kissed her. Kate did not feel the joy that she imagined her first kiss would hold. As he pulled her into a passionate embrace, she firmly pushed him away.

"Darlin'?"

Kate replied breathlessly, "You stole that kiss! I meant to save it for my betrothed."

"Ah, Kate, it was just a kiss, and a very sweet one. I've no regrets."

Kate blushed. "I see. You are presumptuous then."

He jerked his arm away. "Am I? Perhaps you're a bit prudish." Kate's chin quivered, and she blinked back tears. "I should not have said that. I'm sorry. Look, I'm not one to play games. You stir me, Kate, and that kiss was an honest reaction. Obviously, you do not feel the same way about me."

"Of course I'm attracted to you, but I'm a Christian."

"What has that got to do with anything?"

"I believe that when a man and woman love each other, they wed and remain faithful to each other."

"So do I, Darlin'. But marriage is a big step, Kate. I don't recall . . ."

"I also believe in being pure until marriage, to save my kisses for the man I choose to live with for the rest of my life."

"I see. Well, I ain't never heard that one before. That's quite a notion — one that will take a bit to get used to."

They sat still, watching the fireflies flicker. Finally Tanner spoke. "Do you know why I noticed you?" Kate shook her head. "I've always had girls chasing me, trying to latch on to my money, I suppose."

Kate smiled. She knew that was not the only reason women sought Tanner. He could stand on good looks alone.

"You were special, like a rose in a daisy patch. Who wouldn't choose the rare flower over all the others?"

"I don't understand. Why was I different?"

"You were hard to get, Darlin', and now I'm trying to change you. Don't know what came over me. Will you forgive me?" Kate studied his handsome face. When she did not respond immediately, Tanner added softly, "Please."

Tears welled up in Kate's eyes, and a lump formed in her throat.

Tanner reached out for her hand. "Aw, don't cry, Darlin'. Let me make it up to you. How about a picnic next Saturday?"

Kate smiled, "All right."

CHAPTER 3

Sheriff Buck Larson knocked at the door, right on time. He was treating the Tucker House ladies to dinner at the town's new tavern. Buck styled his salt-and-pepper hair slicked back at the sides, and his bushy white sideburns and black mustache provided a striking contrast against his weathered face.

Mattie's eyes lit up when she saw him. "Buck! Good to see ya. Come in." Mattie pointed to a chair in the sitting room and led the way with Buck towering over her, a massive man at six foot one and powerfully built.

Huge creases lined his face, marking him as a man who often smiled. She knew that beneath his calm demeanor he was a man of principle. Stubborn as a mule and stable as the ground beneath his feet, he was not afraid to take any action necessary to keep the law and order in Beaver Creek.

The girls entered the room and found their longtime friend chatting with Mattie. Kate thought, *I wonder why they've never married? Mattie doesn't seem to have any interest in marrying. Maybe she thinks sheriffing is too dangerous.* Romance and marriage intrigued her now that Tanner had entered her life.

"Hello, Sheriff. Sorry to keep you waiting."

"Not at all. My time is yours today." His nod included them all.

"Perhaps," Mattie said with a grin. She knew that if any trouble crossed their paths Buck would lend a hand, for he was not one to shirk a duty.

Buck led them to the wagon, and they rode the mile and a half into town. They could have easily walked, but the sheriff liked to pamper Mattie. Minutes later, he pointed to the valley's newest structure. "There she is: The Lone Wolf."

A wooden sign creaked and groaned between two iron posts where a crude image of the creature's head was etched into the grain. They burst into laughter at the name. Everyone in Beaver Creek knew that there was no lone wolf. The animals were so plentiful that a bounty of fifty cents was offered for each wolf killed in the county.

When they entered the tavern's spacious dining room, Kate's gaze rested on a slight girl with brown hair carrying a pewter water pitcher. The young woman approached and greeted them cheerfully. "Sheriff Larson, nice to see ya. What can I be doin' for ya?"

Buck called her by name. "Elizabeth, this is Mattie Tucker and her daughters, Kate, Annabelle, and Claire. I'll be buying their dinner."

She led them to a small table with four chairs, and Buck pulled up another to make room for the five of them. The inn was pleasant, with two curtained windows facing the street. A shaft of light shot across the room, highlighting an open hearth.

The proprietor's daughter walked with a spring to her step, bringing piping hot roast beef, turnips, and potatoes on pewter plates. A wooden bowl filled with biscuits soon appeared, along with a small platter of butter.

"This is luxury, bein' waited on and such," Mattie said to the sheriff. "Thank ya for givin' us sech a special treat, Buck."

"It's my pleasure."

The heavy door creaked open, and Rose Whitfield and her daughter Melanie entered the room with great commotion. Rose maneuvered across the room, easing her large body between chairs and tables.

"Mattie Tucker! Imagine meeting you here the first time we dropped in, and with the sheriff, too."

"Please join us," Mattie offered. The sheriff shot Mattie a look of disapproval that she disregarded.

"Oh, no! Well, maybe jest to chat a bit." Rose wheezed as she plopped down in a chair that Melanie had pulled up beside the others. The sheriff stretched out his long legs, preparing for a lengthy discourse. Admiring Mattie for her hospitality, he did not interfere.

Melanie began a lengthy narrative involving Kate, something about a pothole and Tanner rescuing her. Annabelle poked Claire, and they burst into a fit of giggles as they watched their older sister squirm.

"Kate, you'll never guess! Ma found out all about Ben Wheeler. Emmett Wheeler is a widower. He has two unmarried sons, Ben and Luke." Melanie cocked her blond curly head to the side and waited for Kate's reply.

Kate smiled. "It's good to have new folks moving into the valley."

Rose interrupted, "My Melanie might even set her cap for one of them. Right handsome they are, the whole lot of them. After she takes her pick, there would be one left over for you, Kate." Rose cackled like an old hen at her own joke, her heavy bosom heaving until she quieted down.

"Kate already has a beau," Annabelle piped up.

"She does now? Who might that be?"

"Mother, I told you Tanner Matthews was courting Kate," Melanie added.

"Oh, that's right. Now that's a man I'm not so sure about. There's rumors going around about those trips he takes to Dayton. Word has it that he gambles and chases women."

"Mother!"

"Like I said, it's jest hearsay, but perhaps it'd be worth checking into. About those Wheeler boys, Annabelle's getting to be about the right age for . . ."

"Rose, please," interrupted Mattie. "There's plenty of time for that." Mattie's stern look dissipated Rose's rambling.

"Very well then."

Kate pitied the Wheeler boys. Ben had seemed like a nice young man to her. She wondered how long it would be until Melanie had her cat claws in him. She shuddered at her own evil thoughts. Anyway, she had her hands full worrying about Tanner.

"I've met the Wheelers. They seem to be a fine family." The sheriff straightened up in his chair as he spoke.

But the matter was dropped when Lillian Denton, the proprietor, came to their table. She had met the sheriff already, and he quickly introduced her to the group. She welcomed them to The Lone Wolf.

"I hope you find Beaver Creek to your likin'," Mattie said.

"I'm sure we will. Everyone is quite agreeable."

"You did sech a wonderful job with the inn. It is very modern." Rose's eyes darted about as she spoke.

"Why thank ya. Now, what kind of pie would ya like for dessert?" She turned toward Rose. "We'll be gettin' your order right away, Ma'am."

Mattie and the girls declined pie, and Buck was soon leading them out of the tavern. "Would you mind if we stroll over to the office just to check things?"

"We'd be delighted," Mattie said, taking his arm while Kate and her sisters followed. As they approached the center of town, they could see Green's Mill, which was situated on the Little Miami close to the juncture of the Beaver Creek. The entire area was humming with the activity of a main thoroughfare. The oldest building was the blockhouse, modified into a jailhouse. Cabins converted into shops lined either side, one of which served as the sheriff's home and office.

"Look! A flatboat!" Claire exclaimed.

"Sure enough!" Buck agreed. "Wonder where they're headed?" They all watched the barge drift close, piled high with barrels of merchandise. One of the passengers waved, and Buck shouted, "What's your cargo?"

The traveler hollered, "Pork, flour, bacon, and whiskey."

"Where you headed?"

"Downriver ta Cincinnati."

A canoe glided by the slow-moving craft, stealing Kate's attention. Two Indians paddled to shore and climbed out. Kate cringed, and her heart beat wildly in her breast.

"The one on the right is Tecumseh," Buck whispered. "He's a Shawnee chief. James Galloway says he speaks good English. His brother, The Prophet, has a mission near Greenville."

The Indians passed with a brisk, elastic step. Tecumseh walked erect and proud, measuring about five feet nine inches.

Annabelle gasped. "Why, he's good looking!"

Kate gave her sister a disgusted sidelong

glance, then riveted her gaze on the Shawnee chief. He wore tanned buckskins and a perfectly fitting hunting frock trimmed in leather fringe. A silver tomahawk hung strapped to his muscular body. It was quite some time before Kate could concentrate on anything except the red-skinned men they had just encountered.

That night Kate's eyes fluttered as she drifted into a fitful slumber and dreamed of childhood days. Six years old again, she was playing in the barn and watching the newborn calf. Caressing her pillow, she rubbed his pink nose, soft as the velvet in Mattie's sewing box. His tongue was rough as sandpaper when he slipped it out to lick her hand. "So long," she murmured. "I gotta go help Ma now."

While Kate dreamed, a storm brewed, and branches squeaked outside her bedroom window. In her vision it was the barn door creaking. She pushed it open and looked around. The wind inflated her bedroom curtains, but she dreamed that her ma's wash was blowing in the breeze with her Sunday dress lying in the mud. "Ma!" Kate called with concern, but her mother was nowhere to be found.

Thunder cracked, then she heard a door

slam and saw her pa running out of the house. He had his rifle across one arm, toting Annabelle and Claire with the other. "Pa! Why are you runnin'?" Fear gripped her body.

"Take your sisters!" he yelled. "Quick! Get down in the root cellar!"

"What's a-matter, Pa?" she cried, grabbing Annabelle and Claire. Her father shoved her into the dark cellar despite her protests, kissed the top of her head, and shut the trapdoor.

Another crack of thunder ripped through the night, and she heard her pa's rifle. Kate put her hand over her ears, but she could still hear the dreadful howling of the Indians.

"No! No!" Kate bolted upright in her bed, shaking and drenched in sweat. She looked around the room. "It was just a dream." She slowly climbed out of bed. Shivering, she stood before her window and watched the rain pelting the earth. Tears tracked her cheeks, and she pulled the window closed with a fierceness that emanated from the terror and hatred that stirred her anew.

CHAPTER 4

Kate opened her eyes but quickly closed them as bright ribbons of sunshine splashed across her face. The sensation was warm and pleasant. Mercifully, the nightmare of the past evening eluded her. Snuggled under the fluffy comforter, she rolled over and savored the moment. *It must be late — the sun is high.* She blinked and took a quick peek. Chatter from below drifted into her room. In a determined motion, she bolted out of bed and pulled on her clothes.

"Morning, Mattie, girls. Glad it's not my turn to fix breakfast or you'd all be starving."

"I'll say," Annabelle grumbled. "We need our nourishment to do all our chores. Why do I have to pull weeds? I'd rather do the cooking."

Mattie shook her finger at Annabelle. "Grab patience by the tail, Child, and hang on with all your might. You'll get your turn ta cook. We all need ta do our share. That's what makes us a family, pullin' together."

"Oh, I know," Annabelle murmured. "I'm sorry."

Kate poured herself a cup of steaming coffee and sat down. She ran her finger around the rim absentmindedly as her thoughts wandered to the recent warnings about Tanner.

Mattie noticed her faraway look. "Thinkin' hard on somethin'?"

"Tanner asked me to go on a picnic Saturday."

"I see. Do ya plan to go?"

Kate nodded and then continued, "I was wondering what you know about him. Do you think there's any truth to Rose's comments at The Lone Wolf?"

"As I recollect, the girls have always chased him. I asked Buck about his trips to Dayton. Tanner goes on business for his pa. Word is out that he had a girl there, but nothin' came of it. All hearsay, mind ya. How do you feel about him, Honey?"

"I'm not sure. He is spoiled and self-centered, but so attractive." Kate giggled. "Those blue eyes and big dimples are hard to resist when he turns on the charm."

"Yes, he is a very good-lookin' lad. Sometimes ya have ta be even more careful with those, Kate. Don't let your heart rule your mind. Ya have to do what ya know is right, even with them blue eyes tellin' ya different."

Mattie wondered if she should tell Kate about her own painful past. She had never planned to share her secret. *Would it keep Kate from making the same mistakes?* Mattie looked around the table and realized that Claire and Annabelle were quietly listening. She decided to wait and see what developed.

Bored with the turn of the discussion, Claire piped up, "I'll go collect the eggs and get started on my chores. Little chicks should be hatching soon." She headed toward the porch for the egg basket.

"I'll help clear the table," Annabelle offered.

Kate and Mattie looked at each other, puzzled. It was natural for Claire to get right at her chores, but not Annabelle. In truth, Annabelle thought she might hear a little more about the charming Tanner Matthews if she stayed in the kitchen. However, the topic was closed.

The week passed quickly, with Annabelle and Claire easily fitting into the summer routine of more chores and free time. Claire checked daily on the setting hens, waiting for those new chicks. Annabelle liked to explore the banks along the creek and watch the beavers at work. The sisters were inseparable. Annabelle provided sparks of creativity to their days while it was usually Claire who managed to keep them out of trouble.

Mattie and Kate went about their chores quietly, in reflection. Mattie worried about Kate's acquaintance with Tanner. Kate looked forward to the picnic but was plagued with a growing sense of uneasiness as well.

On the day of the picnic, Mattie put nervous energy to good use and baked a pie. *Don't know why I'm providin' extra bait for the catch. There he is now, knockin' at the door!* She wiped the wrinkles out of her apron and went to the door, where Tanner stood on the porch. "Come in, Mr. Matthews. I'll be gettin' Kate."

"Thank ya, Miss Tucker." Hat in hand, he waited just inside the door.

Soon Kate, carrying a pie, greeted Tanner. He offered her his arm, and they made their way to his buggy. "Here, let's put that in this basket my mother packed. Looks delicious. Did you bake it?"

"No, I didn't." Kate smiled. "It does look good."

Tanner helped Kate into the buggy, then climbed up and took the reins.

"I hope it doesn't rain again today," said Kate.

"Me, too. I wouldn't miss this picnic, rain or shine."

Kate looked at him warmly. "Where are we going, Tanner?"

"You just wait till you see it, the loveliest spot in Beaver Creek. It's on my property — a small meadow down by the creek with lots of wildflowers and very secluded." He glanced over and noticed Kate's blush. "Don't let that worry you any," he added with one of his most fetching smiles and continued to point out the spring attractions as they rode along.

"Here we are," said Tanner at last. "We have to leave the buggy here and walk the rest of the way." He jumped down and eagerly dashed around the side of the buggy to take Kate by the waist and assist her to the ground. "Just be patient, Darlin', while I tie up the horses."

Kate watched Tanner as he worked. He appeared self-assured. She closed her eyes for just a moment and wished herself to be calm.

Then Tanner grabbed the picnic basket and was back at Kate's side. He offered her his hand, and they walked toward the creek through a wooded thicket. A narrow foot-path indicated that the area was visited frequently. The path sloped downward to the creek, and Kate had to watch her footing so she would not slip.

A breeze kicked up, and she let go of Tanner's hand to fasten her bonnet more securely. In that instant, Kate slid on the steep trail, toppling forward with a shriek. Tanner quickly dropped his basket and reached out to steady her. He held her closely and gazed at her intently.

"Are you all right, Kate?"

Kate laughed nervously. "Yes, I'm fine. Thank you, Tanner."

"Better just let that bonnet fly next time; I'd like to see your hair blowing free anyway." Tanner released her and picked up his basket. "We're almost there. Look!"

"Why, it's lovely! It is the most beautiful place in Beaver Creek! Is all this land yours?"

"Yep. My land and Father's join, making a sizeable spread. This meadow is on the edge of our property. The creek is the boundary line. It's good grazing land."

They spread a blanket on the ground, but the cloth billowed and flapped like a sail at sea. Tanner picked up a couple of rocks and secured the corners. They both ignored the warning signs of an angry sky, behaving as if the day were fine for a picnic. However, the wind got more fierce by the minute.

Tanner managed to secure Kate's hand and started to speak a word of endearment, "Kate, Darlin' . . ." But lightning shot across the sky, followed by a loud crack of thunder that startled them both. They looked up and saw huge, black buffalo clouds rolling in behind them.

Kate smiled. "I think it's going to rain after all. Looks like a storm, too."

"You're right. I don't think we'll have time to take shelter at the house. If we can make it to the buggy, I know of an empty cabin. We could take the horses and wait it out inside."

Quickly, they gathered the picnic fixings. Kate tied her bonnet ribbons securely this time. They started back up the hill, and the return trip proved slower than coming had been. As they reached the buggy and horses, great drops of rain fell, making tiny dimples in the road.

Tanner shoved the basket under the seat and yelled for Kate to throw the blanket over her head. He took the horses, and together they ran toward the deserted cabin, the wind howling and blowing on their backs. Tanner tethered the horses on the protected side of the building and entered the shelter breathlessly.

"Sorry, Darlin', you're all soaked. I reckon we should have cancelled the picnic, but I wanted to see you so much." He gently pulled the blanket down from around Kate and reached up to untie her bonnet. "This is all wet. Better just take it off so you can dry out." He moved his hand to the back of her hair, loosening it to fall freely down her back. Pulling her into a tight embrace, Tanner kissed her passionately.

Kate struggled and pushed him away. "Don't, Tanner! Stop it! I thought you understood. Y–you promised!" He continued to grip her tightly by the arms, angered by her Puritan attitude. "Tanner, you're hurting me!"

"I adore you. I don't want to hurt you." He leaned close, and she turned her face aside. His breath was hot against her cheek.

"Let me go this instant!"

With most women, he just saw what he wanted and took it. A battle raged within him as he struggled to control his frustration, then slowly he released her. "I'm sorry, Kate." The lies slipped smooth as oil off his tongue. "It's just that I'm falling head over heels in love with you." Remembering her convictions, Tanner dramatized by dropping to the floor on his knees. "Marry me, Kate," he pleaded.

"Please get up. The storm is passing, and I'd like to go home."

"Okay, Kate, if that's what you want. But tell me first, I didn't hurt you, did I? Will you forgive me?"

"I'm all right. I just need to think."

"As soon as the storm is over, we'll go. First, listen to what I have to say. I love you and want to marry you."

Half an hour later they headed to Tucker House.

When they arrived, Tanner helped Kate out of his buggy and held her hand a moment longer. "Think about what I said."

Once inside, Kate tried to act calm. She told Mattie that she got caught in the storm and needed to change into dry clothes. Alone in her room, she leaned against the closed door and searched her heart.

CHAPTER 5

Claire and Annabelle were in the henhouse admiring the newly hatched chicks, now two days old. Keeping constant vigil, the hen cackled at the girls and swept her chicks to safety beneath her plump body. They tired easily and slept huddled together looking lifeless. When awake, however, they scrambled about until the anxious hen gathered them safely under her wings. It was an endless routine. The girls were so captivated that they lost track of time.

Claire cooed, "Aren't they just the cutest little things, so soft. I could watch them all day."

Annabelle stretched and yawned. "I think we have."

"Oh, my!" Claire jumped up. "It's getting late! We'd better do the milking and get to the house for supper."

"I hope it's not chicken tonight!" The girls laughed.

Half an hour later they entered the kitchen, where a pleasant aroma greeted them. "Mm, cornbread and beans," said Annabelle, winking at her sister.

Later that evening they sat around the fireplace enjoying each other's company. The June nights were cool, and the fire took off the chill. Mattie was busy sewing lace on a dress for a neighbor. Kate was occupied cleaning out the sewing box and arranging threads and notions. They were listening to Claire and Annabelle's chatter as they played checkers on the board Buck had made for them. The night seemed ordinary enough until a rap at the door startled them.

Mattie placed her sewing aside and moved toward the door. She unlocked the latch and pulled it open.

"Why, Mr. Matthews . . . hello," she said. "Come on in."

"Good evenin', Miss Tucker," said Tanner. "Is Kate here?"

"Yes, come in the sittin' room and pull up a chair. We're jest enjoyin' the fire."

"Yes, the nights are still a bit chilly. Hello, Kate." He gave her a big grin. "Hello, girls." Then he pulled up a chair beside Kate.

"Hello, Tanner," Kate replied softly. She had not found the courage to confide in Mattie about Tanner's behavior. She had been praying for direction; however, she felt confused and uncomfortable in his presence.

"I just got back from a trip to Dayton." Tanner did not realize that was not the best thing he could have said.

"I see," answered Kate sharply. "On a pleasure trip?"

"Why no, Darlin', on business — and a hard trip it was, too."

Mattie interrupted, "What's it like in Dayton now, Mr. Matthews? It's a long while since I've been there."

"Please, call me Tanner. Lively, very lively. All sorts of merchants are setting up shop, and there's all kinds of folks coming in on the Miami from the Ohio River. Folks are moving west in hordes with all their belongings on flatboats." He motioned vigorously with his hands as he spoke. "Others are trading and moving their goods down the river. There's several new inns in town." He blushed and then continued, "And a variety of merchandise. Anything you could be wanting."

"Sounds like a beehive of activity," Mattie said.

"You're right, that's just what it's like." Tanner nodded enthusiastically.

"And the queen bee?" Kate asked.

"Darlin'?" Tanner replied, wondering if he had heard Kate quite right.

"Sounds excitin'," Mattie sighed. "Perhaps we'll take a trip ta Dayton sometime, girls. Would ya like that?"

"Yes! When?" chimed Claire and Annabelle.

"Well, not tonight." Mattie laughed. "It's gettin' ta be your bedtimes. You girls shoo on up to bed. Don't dawdle now! As for me, I think I'll do some readin' in my room. Will ya tend to the fire, Kate, and put out the candles?"

"Yes, Mattie. Good night." The girls made their good nights, and soon all was quiet in the sitting room except for the crackling fire.

"I feel you're upset, Kate," said Tanner, moving his chair closer to her and searching her eyes for his answer. "Is it because I didn't call sooner? I should have sent word that I had to leave town."

"No, Tanner. It isn't that at all," insisted Kate.

"Kate, please look at me." Tanner gently tilted her chin upwards.

A shiver ran through Kate. She quickly moved to the fire, rubbing her arms as if she were cold. Slowly she turned around. Then taking a deep breath, she ventured, "Tanner, you said once that you don't like

44

to play games, so I'd like to be very honest with you if I may."

"That's right, Kate. Go ahead."

"I hear a lot of rumors about your trips to Dayton. I did not want to believe what I heard, but your actions tend to confirm . . ."

Tanner jumped up and stood before her. "What? That I gamble now and then?"

"That you are a womanizer."

Tanner studied Kate before he answered. "I'll admit there may have been some truth to that at one time, but not anymore. I swear it. You're just what I'm needing to become a proper husband. Believe me, Kate, I had good intentions of . . ."

"No!" Kate interrupted him. "I could forgive if you could change, but I don't think you can. You are too practiced."

"I cannot believe that you would hold what's already past against me."

"It's not just that. I don't want to be encouraging you when I don't even know what I'm feeling. You'd better just look somewhere else."

"You think I could just forget you? No! I love you, and my offer of marriage still stands." Kate shook her head sadly, but he continued. "Give me a chance to prove I can change."

"Tanner . . ."

"No. Don't say anything more tonight. Just think about it." He walked to the door, then stopped and looked at Kate with determination. "This isn't good-bye, Darlin'. It's just the beginning." His deep blue eyes spoke words more tender than any that had ever escaped his lips.

"Good night," she said. She wanted to believe him. After the door closed, Kate put out the fire, blew out the candles, and headed upstairs. After much struggling, she fell into a deep sleep.

A few hours later, a terrible ruckus woke Mattie. Jumping out of bed, she ran for the rifle, loaded it, and stole to the front porch to see what was causing the trouble. Something was in the henhouse.

She proceeded cautiously, toting the rifle. Sheriff Larson had taught her to shoot several years back. She was not a very good shot but could scare whatever animal was out there. *If it's a bear . . .* She shuddered to think such a thing. Raising the rifle to her shoulder to take aim, she eyed the culprit. It was just a fox, so she lowered the rifle. Her heart was drumming, rising to the call of battle. She forced herself to relax a moment, and then she made an issue of stomping loudly to the henhouse with her arms swinging wildly like a windmill on wheels. The fox ran off, dragging the old hen with him, and disappeared in the weeds down by the creek.

Mattie peeked inside. It was not a pretty sight. Tomorrow she would deal with it. Now she latched the door and leaned against it for support. Claire and Annabelle would be upset.

Mattie was up at daybreak removing the evidence of the previous night's raid. Feathers were everywhere. She wiped her damp brow with her arm, feeling a little queasy. She knew the trouble was not over. That old fox probably would come sneaking back the first chance he got. Finally, she headed to the kitchen as the house came alive with morning activities.

"Good morning, Mattie. Morning, Kate," Annabelle said as she and Claire entered the kitchen. They sat down and scooted their bench closer to the table.

Kate glanced at Mattie and knew right away that something was wrong. "Mattie, are you feeling all right? What's wrong?"

"Girls, a fox got into the henhouse last night."

"Oh no!" cried Claire. "Are the baby chicks all right?"

"I'm sorry." Mattie shook her head. "They're all dead. When I got out there, it was too late. He took the mother hen and ran off towards the creek."

"Why did he have to kill them? Why not that mean old rooster?"

"I reckon the mother hen put up a ruckus protectin' her chicks and attracted his attention all the more. The chicks were easy pickin's. I guess the hen must've put up a fight."

Claire started sobbing. Annabelle reached to hug her and helplessly looked up at Mattie. That expression broke open the floodgates for Mattie. She joined them in a cry until a knock came at the front door.

Kate jumped up and said, "I'll go." She slipped out and closed the door behind her to provide privacy for her family. There stood James and Frank Potter.

"Hello, boys," said Kate.

"Howdy, Miss Carson. Our ma sent us for the milk. We couldn't get away yesterday."

"That's all right, boys. Let's go down to the springhouse." Kate liked these little fellas. Frank was eleven and James, twelve. Their pa had died a year back, and times were getting real hard for them. They had had to get rid of their milk cows and were one of the families who got their milk at Tucker House. Kate wondered how long they would be able to stay at Beaver Creek. She expected them to move to Dayton, where the boys could earn a living at an early age and support their ma.

"Bye, boys. Tell your ma hello."

"Yes, Miss Carson. Thank ya," said James.

Inside, breakfast was eaten slowly without the usual lively conversation. Kate could hear the scraping of Claire's fork, pushing her food.

Please, Lord, Kate prayed silently, *help us through this morning. Give Claire something good to think about. Help us catch that old fox before he can steal more chickens. May I be an encourager around this house today, Lord.* Then the words of Philippians 4:19 ran through her mind. *"But my God shall supply all your need according to his riches in glory by Christ Jesus."* She smiled. *Thank you, Jesus.*

CHAPTER 6

The icy creek felt so good! The mud oozed up between Claire's toes. *Folks say wading is for boys,* she thought. *But why should girls miss such a pleasure?* She had stripped off her shoes and socks and hiked her skirts, draping them over her arm. *I guess I should have told Annabelle where I was headed.* Her sister loved wading, but Claire wanted to be alone to do some thinking. Plunk! Swish!

"Hey! I didn't see you there, Miss. Did I get you all wet?"

Claire laughed. "Well, I am wet, but it's not your fault." She waded to the edge of the creek and climbed the grassy, sloped bank.

The intruder had a pleasant-sounding voice.

"My name is Ben — Ben Wheeler." He held out his huge, tanned hand and shook her tiny, soft one.

"Nice to meet you. I'm Claire and I live at Tucker House with Mattie Tucker and Annabelle and Kate, who are my sisters. We've all been living together since my folks died."

Ben's heart went out to the little girl. "Oh, I see. I live with my brother, Luke, and my pa. We just moved here a few weeks ago."

"So you're the new neighbor we heard about at The Lone Wolf. Melanie said you almost ran over Kate, and Melanie's ma told her to set her cap for you."

Ben's eyebrows raised in surprise and trepidation at this last remark. Then he chuckled at her innocent expression. "I think I'll like it here if everyone is as friendly as you are, Claire." His eyes wandered far away, taking in the lay of the land. "It's beautiful country."

"Sometimes." A little sob rose in her throat as she recalled the morning's calamity.

"Why do you say that?"

"A fox killed my baby chicks and their mother last night. The fox probably will come back tonight." Claire was trying very hard not to cry, but her mouth twitched uncontrollably, and a tear rolled down her cheek.

"Is there anyone who could catch that fox for you?"

"Catch him? No, we're all afraid. Mattie can shoot, but she was crying this morning. Could you catch him?"

"Perhaps I can. Whoa! Looks like I got what I came for!"

"What's that?"

Plop! Splash! "My supper." He grinned.

Claire wiped away her tears and smiled at the huge shirtless young man. He was tan and muscular. His blue eyes twinkled, and she felt like she could trust him. Something about his freckles made him appealing.

"Here, help me pull him in," Ben offered.

When the fish was safely on shore, Claire giggled. "That was fun! I never fished before."

Ben look astonished. "You mean to tell me that you live here and never fished before? You're pulling my leg."

"No, I'm not. It's menfolk's work and there's no men in our family. We hardly ever have fish for supper, only when Sheriff Larson brings us some."

"Perhaps I could stop by and share my catch after I'm done here and check on that fox for you."

"That would be great!" She proceeded to explain which house was theirs, and Ben assured her he could find his way.

Claire thought she'd better get home before she was missed, so she followed the bank until she came to the place where she had left her socks and shoes. She brushed off her feet, pulled them on without lacing, and hurried home with her news.

That evening, after dinner and before dark, there was a rap on the door.

"I'll get it!" Claire ran to the door. "It's probably him." She flung it open and asked, "You been fishing all this time?"

Ben smiled at the girl with the long blond braids. "No. As a matter of fact, I've been home, cleaned my fish, and had my supper already."

"Well, you sure smell good!"

Ben laughed. "Thank you, Claire."

Mattie came to the door. "Claire, invite our guest in and introduce him."

"Come on in, Ben. This is Mattie."

Mattie reached out and shook his hand. "I'm Mattie Tucker. This is Kate and her sister Annabelle."

"Pleased to meet you all. The name is Ben Wheeler, but please call me Ben, as Claire and I are already on a first-name basis." Ben turned a rosy shade as he continued, "I believe we've met before, Kate."

She smiled, but before she could answer,

Claire piped up, "Didn't you bring us any fish?"

Ben's face reddened even further, and Mattie corrected her daughter. "Claire! Where are your manners, Child?"

Ben quickly said, "Oh, that's all right." Then he addressed Claire, "I thought I should check with Miss Tucker before I came with a pail of smelly fish. Would you like some fish the next time I have a catch?"

"Why, that would be very nice, Ben. We certainly would. We don't fish ourselves, and it would be a real treat."

"Great! It's a promise then."

Claire interrupted. "Kate?"

"Yes," Kate answered.

"I told you he was nice; I like him better than your beau."

Ben looked at Kate, and they blushed as their eyes met. Then Ben burst out in hearty laughter. "It's good to be around children," he said, adding, "You see, my ma died when I was twelve. My brother, Luke, and Pa and I live alone. Luke is eighteen. So we don't have any women or children's chatter at our place."

Kate relaxed. He had such an openness about him, and his sincerity touched her. *Yes, Claire, I like him better, too,* she thought. But she said, "Ben, I'll bet you would enjoy

54

a piece of Mattie's cherry pie then."

"I sure would."

"Me, too," said Annabelle.

Their appetites led them into the kitchen. As they seated themselves around the table, Mattie noticed Kate was stealing glances at their new neighbor, whose back was turned. Ben had brown hair, a ruddy complexion, and the kindest blue eyes. Kate was thinking, *There is something different about his eyes. . . .* He was very tall, even taller than Tanner, with broad shoulders and large hands. He seemed to be genuinely enjoying himself. As Kate sat down to join them at the table, she thought, *I wonder who bakes their bread if it's all menfolk at their place?*

Meanwhile Ben was thinking, *It's good you led me to that fishing hole, Lord. I think these ladies are needing a man's help, and I'd be honored to be your means of helping them.* As he finished his pie, he said, "I thank you for your hospitality. I'm glad to meet my neighbors. The real reason I stopped in was to see if I could help you trap a fox."

"Fox?" Kate asked. "Oh yes! But how?"

"Luke and I will ride back and keep watch. If he doesn't show up tonight, we can set a trap tomorrow."

"Oh, my!" Mattie said. "That's too much

trouble for ya, Ben."

"Not at all; I'd really like to help."

"Well, I have been worried all day," admitted Mattie. "It seems that things have a way of workin' themselves out."

"The Lord provides for His people, Mattie," said Ben.

Kate's head shot up, and a warm sensation rose in her bosom. Did this man know her Lord? *Yes! That's it! I knew there was something special about him,* she thought while gazing into his kind eyes.

CHAPTER 7

Ben was pleased with the choice they had made to move to Ohio. He was delighted that the soil was rich and black, even more fertile than he had imagined. He was contemplating what would make the farm prosper as he trotted along on his horse, Pepper, taking in the lay of the land. Headed home from Beaver Creek, he had picked up supplies they needed for the farm along with the trap for Tucker House. He thought he would drop by now and set the trap.

Reaching Tucker House, he dismounted and secured Pepper to a tree. He intended to go on back to the henhouse and set the trap up right away. Later he would drop by the house and warn the women. As he headed toward the henhouse, a low voice startled him.

He stood still, then ventured a little closer and stopped again. There was Kate, sitting on a bench beneath a big hickory tree. Her head was bowed. Was she crying? He moved forward to approach her, but when he heard her words, he froze in his tracks.

"Today I shall see him again. I dreamed about him last night. He's every inch a man, with a heart as big as all outdoors . . . handsome, and a tower of strength. But best of all, he belongs to You, Lord. Thank you for showing me there are honorable men after all, men worth trusting. Amen."

Ben swallowed hard; now what was he to do? Not meaning to eavesdrop, he had caught her praying about her beau. He quietly backed away. A flood of disappointment washed over him. He sounded nice enough. What was wrong then? He always wanted the best for folks. Why did he feel so low? Maybe he felt ashamed of himself for invading her privacy. *That must be it,* he decided.

Just then, a bloodcurdling scream ripped through the air, stirring him from his reverie. It came from the direction of the creek. Dropping the trap, he raced back to the hickory tree where Kate was rising.

"It's coming from the creek; it's Annabelle!" she shouted. Ben flew by her. The yard sloped downward, past the other buildings to the creek. He ran toward the water.

Kate picked up her skirts and followed close behind.

"Head for the water!" screamed Ben. The sight was awful. Annabelle was covered with bees, which were swarming everywhere. He swooped Annabelle up into his strong arms and, swatting at the bees, charged ahead for the creek. "Come on, get in the water," he yelled to Kate. Bees were stinging both of them by now. The buzzing was horrendous. Ben dunked Annabelle several times. "Dip under," he yelled to Kate. She plunged under. Each time she came up gasping, the bees landed on her head. They stormed madly, a small winged army.

Finally, the bees were avenged. They slowly dispersed, flying in bands back to the tree that held their honeycomb. Annabelle was choking and crying hysterically. Ben held her close, speaking soothingly, "It's all right now, Annabelle. They're all gone." He carried her to Kate, who stood in the water totally soaked, her dress clinging to her, and her hair drenched and dripping in little ringlets. "Are you all right, Kate?" he asked.

"Yes," she said. "Is Annabelle?"

"Her eyes are swelling shut. We'd better get some mud packs on these welts on her face right away." He gently laid her down on the bank, but she clung tightly to his drenched shirt, sobbing. Ben went to work, quickly scooping handfuls of mud and patting it onto the welts. "The ones on her face are covered. It will draw out the poison. Run to the house and tell Mattie, Kate. Then come back and we'll take care of the stings you got."

Kate jumped up and raced for the house. "Mattie! Mattie!" she screamed as she approached.

Mattie came running out of the house and beheld Kate's soaked clothes and dripping hair. "What's the matter?" she asked.

"Annabelle got into a beehive," Kate gasped. "Ben has her down at the creek. He's putting mud on the welts."

"Oh no!" Mattie exclaimed. They both ran back to the creek. By this time, Annabelle had calmed down. The mud felt cool and had eased the pain. Mattie rushed to tend her.

Ben went over to Kate. "Come on, let's get some mud on your welts." By the time they finished plastering themselves, they looked like two mud pies.

"Thank you, Ben." Kate shivered. "Come up to the house; let's see if we can find some dry clothes for you."

"You don't have in mind to put me in a dress, do you?" he teased.

"I was thinking more in the line of a blanket." She blushed.

"Well, I don't know about that."

Minutes later he sat at the kitchen table wrapped in a quilt while Mattie brewed coffee. She had left Annabelle resting comfortably in her bed, sipping hot tea and receiving sympathy from Claire. Kate was changing into dry clothes.

When Kate came down the stairs and entered the kitchen, she heard Ben say, "We got here too late to plant; the land had to be cleared and prepared. So we started on our cabin and barn first. With the shelter built now, we've started to work the land."

"Sounds like hard work," said Mattie. "I hate to have ya bothered with our problems, too."

"It's really no bother. Pa says helping folks is the most important part of living. People in Virginia chipped in and helped us when our ma died."

"I'm sure your pa is a very decent man; we'd like ta meet him and your brother. We're having some neighbors for dinner Sunday. Would ya like ta come and bring your family?"

"Sure thing! Never turn down home cooking."

Kate looked at his huge hands. She could

not imagine him stirring a pot of stew or pouring coffee, but she could imagine him chopping wood, felling trees, and clearing land. Then she realized they were staring at her and had asked her a question. She blushed. "I'm sorry. What did you say?"

"You feeling all right, Kate?" Ben asked.

"Fine." She nodded.

When Ben's clothes were dry enough to wear, he prepared to leave. He still had to set the trap. "Don't forget the bread I baked for you," Kate reminded him. "See you on Sunday."

"I probably won't be stopping in before then unless I catch the fox. I'll let you know if we get him."

"Hmm," Mattie muttered as she listened to the sound of his horse riding away.

Kate glanced her way. "What's wrong, Mattie?" She rubbed a welt on her shoulder.

"It's a tricky situation," Mattie replied. "They're a family of menfolk, and we're a bunch of womenfolk. We could be helpin' each other, but we don't want them to think we're chasin' them; and we don't want people ta start talkin'. I invited them to dinner."

"Well, let's invite others, too. I know! Let's invite the sheriff."

Mattie laughed. "That doesn't fix it; that

still makes all menfolks."

"I know," Kate said. "Let's invite the Potters — James, Frank, and their ma."

"Hmm." Mattie studied a moment and then replied, "I guess that would be fittin'. Well then, it's settled. Now, I'd better go check Annabelle." Mattie started to walk away. She glanced back, and there stood Kate, rubbing a painful welt on her neck with a sweet smile on her lips.

CHAPTER 8

Sunday morning Tucker House teemed with activity and excitement in anticipation of the company coming that day. Perfect pies waited on the table. Mattie fried chicken, and already prepared were freshly baked bread and butter. There were greens from the garden, deviled eggs, potatoes and gravy, beans and hominy, and strawberries and cream.

Annabelle and Claire finished setting the table and perched on the porch like two little sparrows, waiting for the folks to arrive. Both girls were now admirers of Ben. He had won Claire's heart when he taught her to fish and Annabelle's when he rescued her.

The first buggy approached, and James, Frank, and Mrs. Potter arrived. The boys seated themselves beside the girls on the porch. Annabelle captivated them immediately, telling of her horrible adventure with the bees and proudly pointing to the spots on her face. Mrs. Potter bustled past them into the house, carrying a bowl of rice pudding.

The sheriff and the Wheelers arrived at the same time and made their own introductions. Then Mattie came out and invited everybody inside, where they sat down to the delicious meal.

"What, no honey?" teased Ben as he winked at Annabelle.

"That's what I was doing," she exclaimed. "Looking for their honey."

"I thought so." He smiled. "You're looking very good, considering what an ordeal you've been through."

After the tale had been told about the bees, Sheriff Larson said he had big news to share. "We'll be getting some important visitors around Independence Day."

"Really, who?" Mattie looked at the sheriff with admiration as she posed her question.

"Ohio's Gov. Edward Tiffin. He will be speaking at the Independence Day doin's in Dayton and spending the night in Beaver Creek on his way. I reckon there will be celebrating in Dayton. The militia will parade with fifes and drums and fire a volley followed by a blast from a cannon. The governor will speak. There will be a hog roast and drinking and toasting, then a dance in the evening."

"It's a wondrous thing we have, this freedom of ours," said Mr. Wheeler.

"Yes, and Ohio's future looks bright since we finally have our statehood," the sheriff added.

"What have you heard of Jeremiah Morrow?" Emmett Wheeler asked while he scratched his chin. "Is he a man to be trusted?"

"Oh, yes," the sheriff quickly answered. "Why, he'll make a fine representative for Ohio. He already has done so much. . . ."

Claire interrupted the sheriff as he stopped to take a sip of water. "Will we celebrate here in Beaver Creek, or will we go to Dayton?"

Mattie turned to the sheriff, and he replied, "I guess we should have our own celebration, Claire, for those folks who can't go to Dayton."

"Yeah! Yeah!" the children all cheered.

Buck thought aloud, "The Coopers of the General Store, and the Bennetts and Dentons who own the inns ought to be in charge. I'll talk to them about it."

Luke asked about the merchants in Beaver Creek, and the sheriff was proud to give him information on his little town. Kate was listening and dreaming. *Luke looks a lot like Ben. I wouldn't know he was the youngest. Ben is twenty and Luke eighteen. They have the same broad shoulders and freckles, only Luke's hair is blond while Ben's is brown.* Emmett Wheeler had white hair, so she could not tell if Ben favored his pa or ma. Now Mr. Wheeler was talking.

"We lived in Virginia, where I preached while I raised my family. The state got overcrowded, and the prices kept going up. Farms gave way to plantations. Folks mostly wanted to raise tobacco. Ben was interested in farming and heard about the sale of land in Ohio. A man could buy a hundred sixty acres for a dollar an acre and pay it off in four years. Well, the long and the short of it is, we came west."

"So you're a Virginian," exclaimed the sheriff. "A lot of good men come from Virginia."

"I suppose you're referring to President Jefferson. Yes, a good man indeed," Mr. Wheeler answered.

"Well, the Federalists probably wouldn't agree with us," said Sheriff Larson.

"No, that they wouldn't!" Emmett Wheeler laughed. "But Jefferson's got good principles. He tries to keep tyranny from seeping into the government, and he stands behind the farmers. He promotes education, hopes to better inform folks and let the intellectual govern rather than the rich."

Buck nodded. "Yes, but he rides the fence when it comes to states' rights."

"I think he just sees both sides and tries to do what is best for the country and the states," answered Mr. Wheeler. "I suppose we should change the subject before you ladies throw us out," he added with a chuckle.

"What happened to your church when you left?" Mary Potter asked.

"There was plenty of time for folks to get another preacher. I think I'll let Luke do the preaching in this family from now on, unless God changes my mind."

"Luke?" she asked.

"Yes, Luke plans to help us get our farm going, and then go back East for more schooling. He wants to preach, and Ben and I will farm."

Luke blushed. "Yes, that's what I want to do. Don't know another man whose tracks I'd rather follow than my father's."

Sheriff Larson said, "I heard there is a new university in Athens, Ohio."

"I'll check into that, Sir."

After dinner the children took a jaunt to

the creek, and the men visited in the sitting room while the ladies cleared the table and did the dishes. By the time the women finished, the sheriff and the Wheelers seemed very comfortable sharing together. As the ladies entered the sitting room, Ben was thinking, *I'm surprised Kate didn't have her beau here today.* Then he heard his pa saying, "Do you know of someone who would want to cook, wash, and clean for a bunch of menfolk a couple days a week?"

Mary Potter piped up, "I'd be willin' to work at your place a couple days a week. Since the boys' pa died, it's been hard to make ends meet. I've been wonderin' how long it would be before we'd have to move to the city so the boys could get some work."

"It'd be hard work at our place," Mr. Wheeler warned with a smile.

"I'm used to hard work," she said anxiously.

"Very well, Mrs. Potter, it's a deal then." Mr. Wheeler stood up and held out his hand. She smiled, and they shook on it.

On the way home that evening, Mr. Wheeler was telling his sons how faithful God was in finding them a widow to help around the place.

"It sure will be nice," agreed Luke.

"That Kate sure is a pretty one, boys."

"Oh, Father," Luke spoke, "you know I won't be settling down for a long time with schooling ahead."

"She already has a beau," added Ben thoughtfully.

"Strange he wasn't there today." Mr. Wheeler glanced sidelong at Ben, whose wrinkled forehead gave him the impression of being disturbed about something. Mr. Wheeler had observed Ben's quiet side all day. As he pondered on the meaning of it, he said quietly, "We still got chores to do before dark, boys."

Back at Tucker House, darkness swallowed up the light where Mattie and the sheriff sat on the porch visiting.

CHAPTER 9

June passed without a fuss to make way for the pomp and splendor of July, whose gown of golden glory was woven with threads of independence, honor, and liberty. She touched hearts with the message of freedom and stirred the townsfolk into action. They prepared for the Independence Day celebration with great anticipation.

During this time, Tanner continued to drop in occasionally at Tucker House, and Kate endeavored to discourage him, but in vain. She turned down his invitation to the Independence Day picnic but promised to see him there.

Gov. Edward Tiffin arrived at Beaver Creek on schedule. Much ado was made. All the townsfolk gave him a hearty welcome. He gave a short speech, a portion of the one that he would be delivering in Dayton on the following day. The menfolk gathered around and listened hungrily, lap-ping up every morsel of political news.

The next morning, his departure ushered in the long-awaited Independence Day. There would be a picnic at noon by the creek and games in the afternoon. Toward nightfall, everyone would gather on the main street in Beaver Creek for speeches, more celebrating, and dancing.

Sheriff Larson stopped by to pick up the ladies at eleven o'clock, right on time. Spirits were high with expectation as they climbed into his wagon. Mattie perched on the front seat with the sheriff, and the girls climbed into the back.

Kate picked a few pieces of straw off her skirt and flicked them over the side while watching the ground, parched and dusty, passing by beneath her. The girls at Tucker House dressed nicer than most with Mattie's trade being such as it was. Kate had on a new blue dress capped with a round white collar. Her shiny, black hair hung to her waist and curled at the ends. A few short strands worked free and curled about her face. Blue ribbons intertwined her hair and fashioned a bow in the back. Her white bonnet sat on her lap like a cloud spewing showers of blue ribbons.

Soon they heard the sound of laughter and chatter emanating from the folks gathered along the banks of the Beaver Creek. Then the site of the fete came into view, a small grassy meadow that glimmered in the sun. It was surrounded on three sides by shady glades fringed in forest, and a shady creek bank on the fourth. The area brimmed with activity.

The Wheelers had just arrived and came to greet them as their wagon rolled to a stop. Mr. Wheeler chatted with Mattie and Buck as Ben rushed to help Annabelle and Claire off the wagon. Luke reached up to offer Kate a hand, and then grabbed her by the waist, whirling her to the ground. She felt light as a feather in his iron arms.

Annabelle and Claire dashed off to find the friends that they had not seen since school. "That'll be the last we see of them until it's dinner time," Kate said laughingly.

"They make a lively pair," said Ben warmly.

"You know they're both crazy about you."

"Yes, and I love the attention."

Ben and Luke helped Kate carry pies, potatoes, and strawberries to the tables. "What did you fellas make?" she teased.

"Why, Mrs. Potter will be bringing our share," Ben offered.

"Are you happy with your arrangement?"

"Happy as a lark!" Ben said.

"I'll say," agreed Luke. "She's a great cook, and the place is starting to seem like a home."

"I'm glad," Kate said. "How is your farmland coming along?"

"Fine. I believe we'll be ready to plant next spring for sure," said Luke.

"If Luke would just do his share," teased Ben. They playfully punched at each other.

As they walked on, Kate introduced them to friends. Blankets and quilts were being spread; children were running and laughing, dodging in and out of the crowd of adults where folks shared the latest bits of gossip.

As usual, Sheriff Larson was the one in charge of speaking. He climbed onto a wagon and tried to get folks' attention. Some of the older boys came to his aid with whistles, loud and shrill. Finally the crowd settled down, and he spoke. "Good morning, friends and neighbors! It's good to get together and celebrate the freedom and birth of our country, the United States of America!" There was clapping and hooting all around the crowd.

"Three cheers for Ohio!" someone shouted. "Hurray for statehood!" another yelled.

When it finally grew quieter, the sheriff

said, "Emmett Wheeler will pray, and then everyone help themselves. There's water on the wagon at the end of the last table and don't forget to get some of that tasty pork so generously donated by the Bennetts." Everyone clapped and some whistled, then all quieted down as Mr. Wheeler prayed.

"Shall we get in line?" Kate asked.

Ben nodded. "Sure, Kate. Come on, Luke. Looks like a real feast."

This is going to be a fine day, Kate thought. She was enjoying the Wheeler brothers' company and easy ways. Just as the line moved again and they started to fill their plates, she felt a hand on her elbow. She turned, and there stood Tanner.

"H–hello, Tanner," Kate stammered. She blushed scarlet.

"Hello, Darlin'," he said.

Kate stiffened. Ben thought she looked embarrassed. "You remember the Wheelers, don't you, Tanner?"

"Of course, Darlin'." Tanner reached out to shake their hands. His charming smile was intact, but his handshake told a different story. It was stiff and unfriendly.

As they made their way through the tables laden with all the good foods, Kate hardly knew what she was dipping onto her plate.

Tanner had squeezed between Kate and the Wheelers and was whispering something in her ear. Then he said loudly, "May I talk to ya a minute, Darlin'?"

Ben quickly said, "Excuse us," and nodded a good-bye to Kate.

Tanner led her the opposite direction and stopped under a tree. "Is this why you wouldn't come to the picnic with me?"

"What do you mean?"

"Got your eye on one of them Wheelers?"

Across the meadow, Ben and Luke observed the scene. Luke said with a sheepish grin, "It looks like we got Kate into an argument with her beau."

"I feel mighty bad about that," sighed Ben sadly.

"Don't worry, Ben. They'll make up soon enough."

As soon as the food had a little time to settle, groups started gathering here and there, preparing for the games. First came the children's games — various relays and races for all ages. Then some of the older men went down to the creek for a fishing contest. Ben wanted to ask the sheriff about the shooting match but thought he should stay clear of Kate. He did not want to cause trouble; it was the Wheelers' way to try to live peaceably with all folks.

Sheriff Larson told Mattie that he would not be able to hold up his head in town unless he participated in the shooting match. She encouraged him to enter and moved her blanket close to watch. Ben and Luke spied Buck, and they all entered together.

The first shot was Sheriff Larson's, and he was a little low and to the right of the bull's-eye. Ben and Luke were not nearly as close. Carl Hawkes hit the bull's-eye right on.

During the applause Tanner handed Kate a posy. She clutched it in surprise. Then he marched up to the Wheelers with a threat. "Stay away from Kate," he said straightway.

"We're just neighbors; there's nothing for you to worry about," Ben replied.

"Look, you'll be sorry if I catch you together again," Tanner warned. Then he took his shot. It was close, but too high. Tanner's strutting took the pleasure out of the contest for Ben.

When the target looked like a sieve and all was done, Sheriff Larson won by getting the last two shots into the bull's-eye. Carl Hawkes piped up, "If somebody had to beat me, I'm glad it's the sheriff we got protectin' the town!" But he was interrupted by screams coming from the creek.

Everyone looked, and a crowd gathered.

Kate got there just as twelve-year-old Sammy Hawkes dove into the middle of the creek. "What? Why, that's my Sammy! What's goin' on?" Carl Hawkes yelled.

"It's little Zach, the Greens' baby boy," a lady nearby sobbed. "He's disappeared under the water."

Mr. Hawkes was just about to dive into the water when Sammy emerged, gasping. "I–I f–found h–him," he stuttered.

Mr. Hawkes lifted the small boy from his son and hurried to the bank, where he quickly worked over him. Sammy and the Greens gathered around with a crowd of friends pressing in behind them.

The baby kicked and sputtered. After a moment Carl handed him to his ma. "He's breathin'! Oh, my baby's breathin'! Thank the Lord," Rose Green sobbed as she cradled her son in her arms and rocked him back and forth.

David Green turned to Sammy and his pa. Deeply moved, he embraced them each in turn and thanked them for saving the boy. Sammy was smiling from ear to ear.

Kate saw Claire standing not too far away with teary eyes and went to her. "I'm so happy," Claire said, "for baby Zach, but most of all for Sammy!" Claire felt compassion for her friend Sammy. She had often brought stories home from school about his stuttering problem. The older boys teased him, and it saddened her.

"Yes, he's a real hero," Kate agreed.

After that, the afternoon seemed to wind down, and before long, everyone was packing up to head home. Tanner led Kate to the sheriff's wagon and made her promise to dance with him later in the evening. As she watched him walk away, she noticed Ben and Luke were not lacking for friends.

They stood in a group of folks, laughing and talking. Melanie Whitfield whispered in Ben's ear, and he nodded and grinned. She recalled what Mrs. Whitfield had predicted about Melanie setting her cap for one of the Wheeler boys.

As the wagon rolled down the shady road again, it seemed to hit every rut and bump in the road. With each bump, Kate grew angrier.

CHAPTER 10

Late that same afternoon, the Tucker House ladies walked into Beaver Creek to take part in the street festivities. The road was hot and dusty, and they wore their best clothes with shawls draped over their arms. As they entered the outskirts of town where all the buggies and wagons were left, they heard a loud bong. Their excitement mounted.

On Main Street, they were met by the familiar smells of beaver pelts and tanned leather goods, mixed with the repugnant odors of livestock, sweating men, and cigar smoke. Occasionally the ladies' sweet smell of lavender lingered.

The bong was a huge drum. A wooden platform was erected in front of Cooper's General Store. Various merchants and townsfolk gave speeches on freedom and liberty. The people addressed the political events that Gov. Edward Tiffin had introduced. They discussed Ohio's statehood and plans for their town. There was even talk of locks and canals on the Ohio River.

By six o'clock the speeches were concluded. Drums sounded and men fired rifles into the air. They grabbed their women and swung them around and around, like colorful twirling tops. There was hooting and hollering, and it all ended with rounds of applause.

Kate noticed several men gathering around the big bonfire site to ignite the fires for light and warmth when the evening chill set in. Various shopkeepers set out candles and hung oil lamps from rafters. As darkness fell, they created an enchanting setting.

The fiddlers consisted of two farmers, one shopkeeper, and a half-grown youngster. As they started warming up, Kate stopped to watch.

Kate noticed Ben Wheeler asking Melanie Whitfield to dance. Disappointed, she quickly looked away. Luke saw her moping. He glanced around, and Tanner was not in view, so he asked her to dance. Colorful dresses made a beautiful sight, full and swaying like a myriad of flowers floating in a pond. When the dance was over, Luke thanked her and politely excused himself.

Kate watched Mattie dance with the sheriff. She hummed and tapped her feet to the music. Claire, Annabelle, and Dorie Cooper were sitting on the porch in front of Cooper's General Store, enjoying themselves and watching the crowd and the dancing. She waved to them.

Then Tanner asked her to dance. He held her possessively and whispered in her ear, "You look beautiful tonight, Darlin'."

Ben danced a set each with Annabelle and Claire. Kate was studying his graceful moves with her sister when suddenly he turned and caught her gazing his way. He gave her a wink and a smile. Kate reddened and quickly looked up at Tanner. The gesture had escaped his notice for his attention focused on Elizabeth Denton across the way. Kate noticed that his eyes were red and realized that he had been drinking.

"Are you as thirsty as I am?" Tanner asked.

Kate nodded, seeing her chance to get out of his grip. "I could use a drink." Tanner led her to the edge of the crowd, and they strolled along the wooden walkway that ran in front of the shops.

"Wait here, Darlin'. I'll be right back."

Meanwhile, Ben and Luke happened on each other and stopped to talk. "Having a good time?" asked Luke.

"Who wouldn't?" his brother replied.

"A lot of pretty girls," Luke drawled, smiling.

"Now remember your goals," Ben chided.

"Sometimes it's hard," Luke admitted. "Say, look over there! Tanner is deserting Kate."

Ben winced. "He's drunk, the scoundrel! Think he'd carry his threat through?"

"Are you afraid of him?"

"Of course not!"

"Well, what are you waiting for? I've had a dance with Kate myself."

That was all the prodding Ben needed. He headed toward Kate, who stood in a small gathering of young folks. "Hello, Ben! Have you met everyone here?"

"Yes, I believe I have." He nodded to the others and smiled. Then he added, "Would you like to dance, Kate?"

The question roused a tingling sensation like teeny, tiny soldiers marching up and down her spine. She heard herself reply ever so softly, "Yes." Then she was in his arms, gliding as if on air to the movements of the dance.

"Enjoying yourself, Ben?"

"Yep. Folks are friendly and know how to have a good time."

"I noticed you are making many friends," she said. Suddenly, she was too hot and feeling dizzy. "Could we walk a spell?" she asked.

"Sure, Kate." He led her toward the walkway. "Do you want to tell me about it?" he asked. "I don't want to push you, Kate. But you know I'm your friend, and I can tell something's bothering you."

The words were barely out of his mouth when they turned the corner and came upon a sight that shocked them completely. There was Tanner with another woman in his arms.

Kate gasped and Tanner released the young lady he was kissing. "Tanner! E–Elizabeth!" Kate stammered. She did not wait for an answer but turned on her heels and fled, with Ben following close behind.

"Wait, Kate!" Tanner hollered. He saw it was no use. He'd best let her cool off. He turned to Elizabeth with a sheepish grin. "Dance?"

Ben caught up with Kate and grabbed her arm. "Kate!" Ashamed, she turned toward him with her eyes glued to the ground. "I know it hurts," he said.

"No, not really." She laughed a hollow laugh. "I was trying to break it off for weeks anyway."

"You don't care for him then?"

"No. At first I was attracted to him . . .

but I soon realized what he was like, and now I cannot tolerate him."

Ben tenderly wiped Kate's tear away from her cheek. "Tanner may be a fool, but I'm not. May I escort my good friend for the rest of the evening?"

Kate smiled. "I guess we didn't finish our dance, did we?" Ben led her through the crowd and took her in his arms, moving to the rhythm of the music. The fiddler started to play some familiar tunes, and the people clapped and sang along.

All of a sudden, Ben was stumbling awkwardly, falling against some ladies who moved out of the way screaming and shrieking. Kate gasped and looked at Ben questioningly, and then in an instant she realized that Tanner had pushed him.

Ben soon had his balance and turned to face Tanner. A crowd gathered around, and the fiddlers stopped playing. "I thought I told ya to keep away from my girl!" Tanner yelled in a drunken drawl.

"She's not your girl, Tanner," Ben said firmly.

Tanner took a wild swing at Ben, and Ben grabbed his arm in midair and held it for an instant. Jake Hamilton was standing nearby and shouted to his friend, "Aw, come on, Tanner. Let it be!"

Tanner struggled free and lurched at Ben again, swinging wildly and hitting Ben with several punches. His eyes were red with fury and whiskey, and he looked like a mad bull. Ben stood tall, letting Tanner hammer away at him until Tanner hit him with a blow to the stomach. Just as Ben hunched over, struggling for air, the sheriff intervened, hitting Tanner in the temple and sending him sprawling to the ground.

"I hate to hit a man when he's drunk," the sheriff said. "Take him home, Jake."

Then the sheriff turned to Ben. "Are you all right?" he asked, watching Ben and wondering why he had not defended himself.

"I'll be fine," Ben said.

After the fight was over, the fiddlers started playing again. Slowly the people dispersed, but Kate just stood there, the horror of the scene besetting her like a big, dark cloud. "I'm so sorry, Ben," she cried.

"It's all right, Kate. It's not your fault."

The throng of lively dancers was fast closing in on them. "If you'd like to walk me home, we can clean up your cuts," Kate suggested. "Your face is bleeding."

Ben took her hand, leading her through the crowd. Melanie was watching as they walked away. "So much for Tanner Matthews and Kate Carson," she mumbled and marched away in a huff.

When they reached the dirt road that led to Tucker House, Kate broke the silence. "Ben?"

"Yeah?"

"Why did you let him hit you without striking back?"

"Why, Kate, fighting is not my way; I'm not a violent man," he said softly.

"I thought all men had to be tough to survive today . . . out here in the West, I mean."

"I reckon it ain't any different today than any other time, when it comes to living," Ben mused. Then he grinned. "I didn't say I wasn't tough, did I?"

Kate didn't respond as she was taking it all in, trying to understand the meaning of it.

"A man shows strength in restraint," Ben said simply.

"I don't understand. What do you mean?"

"It's the way I believe. It's part of my faith. Jesus instructs in His Word, 'Ye have heard that it hath been said, An eye for an eye, and a tooth for a tooth: But I say unto you, That ye resist not evil: but whosoever shall smite thee on thy right cheek, turn to him the other also.' That's not an easy thing to do, Kate."

Kate looked up at him with wonder in her eyes. Although it was too dark to see him clearly, she understood. With this new insight, she saw him clear as a bell, this huge strong man with the freckled bleeding face and tender heart. He had said he was her friend. She realized this was indeed a precious thing.

Walking on in the dim moonlight, his presence by her side seemed comfortable, and she felt very safe beside this man who practiced nonresistance. As they walked on in silence, Kate wondered why this was. Then she realized it was because he was a man of God and she trusted God.

At the same time, Ben was considering, *She couldn't have been praying about Tanner that day. I wonder who it was then?*

CHAPTER 11

Mattie and Kate did their washing outside under the trees with their tub near the springhouse so they did not have to carry the water so far. A clothesline hung close by. They took turns scrubbing with lye soap and hanging the clothes on the line or over bushes to dry. There was plenty to do today. Whenever there was a special event, it meant extra wash. However, sharing each other's company always made their work seem lighter. Kate was pondering on this when familiar words ran through her mind.

"Come unto me, all ye that labour and are heavy laden, and I will give you rest. Take my yoke upon you, and learn of me; for I am meek and lowly in heart: and ye shall find rest unto your souls. For my yoke is easy, and my burden is light."

"Mattie?"

"Yes, Kate?"

"When do you think we'll have a church in Beaver Creek?"

"Why, I don't know, Kate. You'd really like that, wouldn't ya?"

"Yes, I would. I read my Bible, and sometimes the words I've read go running through my mind, and I don't fully understand them. I wish there was someone to explain them to me. Mattie?"

"Yes?"

"Don't you believe in God?"

"Well, sure I do, Kate. It's jest that . . . I have some painful memories, and I don't feel like He ever cared much about me. But if it's important to you, why don't ya talk to Emmett Wheeler about it? It's a shame ta have his talents wastin'. I suppose there are others who feel the same way you do, Kate."

"Really? I wonder if he'd consider preaching? I'm sure we could find someplace to meet. Oh, Mattie, thanks for the idea! I will talk to him! Perhaps I'll talk to Ben first."

"Now there's a fine fella," Mattie said. "By the way, what were him and Tanner fightin' about last night?"

Kate blushed. "I didn't want to worry you, Mattie, but Tanner is a womanizer. The day of the picnic when it rained, he took me into a deserted cabin. And, well . . . he tried for my affections. But I refused him, and he was rough with me."

"Oh, no!" Mattie let the wet clothes slip from her hands into the tub of water. Her face turned white with fear, and her hands clenched. "I've failed ya, Kate," she cried.

"Oh, no, Mattie! It's not your fault at all!"

"Yes. Yes, it is. I should have shared somethin' with ya the day you asked me about Tanner. I'm so sorry, Kate." Mattie's shoulders shook, and she started to weep.

Kate rushed to her and knelt at her side. "He didn't hurt me, Mattie," she quickly explained.

"Are . . . are you sure?" Mattie asked.

"I believe Jesus protected me because Tanner was strong enough to do what he wanted."

"Thank God!" Mattie moaned. "I feel so guilty." The words poured out. "I should have told ya what . . . what happened to me."

"Tell me, Mattie," Kate urged.

Mattie was silent for a long moment as Kate waited patiently. Then she painfully and slowly began to share some of the secret from deep within. "There was no one I could talk ta. Ya see, my father was a preacher. He was very strict. My mother was a very quiet and shy person, totally controlled by my father. She didn't tell me anythin' about fellas and havin' babies and what to watch for. When I went to her with questions, she jest brushed me off, tellin' me not ta think of such things!"

Mattie paused a moment, and then continued. "There was a young man who lived nearby, and he started ta come around. My father ran him off. I didn't know why. I think my father knew what he was like, but he didn't explain it to me or anythin'. Instead he yelled at me and accused me of not bein' the proper, chaste young lady I was to be.

"Well, the young man and I had secret meetin's. It wasn't too hard, since he lived close. We met in the woods nearby, or after dark he'd come over, and I'd go out ta the barn to be with him. He made me feel loved, which I never felt from my family. He talked of elopin' and havin' a place of our own. I didn't know he was lyin' to me. I–I b–became p–pregnant."

Mattie sobbed uncontrollably now, and Kate held her. "Oh, Mattie, you poor thing," she said. "What happened?"

"I told him." Mattie sighed. "He said we'd get married and not ta worry, but he left town, and I never saw him or heard from him again. I never even knew where he'd gone."

"What did you do?"

"I told my parents about the baby. My father was furious. He said I was a harlot, and he didn't want anythin' ta do with me. I was to get out of his house. My mother took me aside and said that I should go and stay with my sister. So I went to Big Bottom where Beth lived. She took me in."

"Big Bottom!" Kate exclaimed. "Then that's how you found us?"

"I reckon so. . . ." Again Mattie paused, wondering how much to share. She quickly concluded, "After I had the baby, my sister raised her because she didn't have any children of her own. She was good ta me."

"What happened to your baby?" Kate interrupted.

"The Indians that killed your folks . . ." Mattie could not finish, and Kate, thinking that she understood, did not ask any more about it. She had her own memories of that Indian raid. Both women were kneeling on the ground, holding each other and reliving that time.

Finally Kate said, "I'm so sorry, Mattie. You've been such a good mother to me."

"Kate, I jest want ta spare ya the mistakes I made. If a young man really loves ya, he'll have proper intentions. He'll save his advances for your weddin' night. He'll respect and honor ya."

"Like Ben. He's that kind of man."

"Ya like him?"

"When I'm around him, my heart pounds as if it's going to explode. I'm afraid he's going to discover . . . I don't want to lose him as a friend."

"Jest give it time, Kate. Ben is a good man. He won't go rushin' into anythin'. Did ya tell Ben about Tanner?"

"Just that I wanted to break it off with him. That was after we happened upon Tanner with Elizabeth Denton in his arms."

"Oh, Kate! I'm sorry!"

Kate shrugged. "Tanner attacked Ben because he was jealous. Ben told him to leave me alone. Tanner was so drunk. I don't know if he even remembers or if he understood. I don't know if he'll stay away."

"Well, I won't let him in the next time he comes around here! The scoundrel!"

"With everyone protecting me, I guess it'll be all right. Ben said he'd keep him away, too. He said that he was my friend and I could trust him."

"It's good ta have someone to trust. That's the way I feel with Sheriff Larson."

"There's someone else you can trust, too, Mattie."

"Yeah? Who's that?"

"God. I understand now why you don't want to have anything to do with Him, because of your father. But that wasn't God's fault. Your father was in the wrong. Look at people like the Wheelers; then you get a better picture of what God's like. Sometimes it's best not to look at anyone except God Himself. We're all just human after all."

"How do ya know what God's like, Kate?"

"Well, since I was little, He's always been there for me. My parents were Christians, and they taught me to pray. Even as a little girl, when I prayed I knew He heard me, and I knew He cared for me. During that Indian raid, I felt His presence in such a real way. I felt His hand on my shoulder. I never told anybody that but I knew it was Jesus. I even said, 'Jesus, is that you?' And he said, 'Lo, I am with you always, Child.' He's my best friend, Mattie. He's been faithful to me. I wish Annabelle knew Him. She was just too little at the time, I guess. But if we had a church . . . if she could know him, and Claire, and you, Mattie . . ."

"Well, I guess if God wants me to know Him, He'll have ta make the first move. Maybe He will, Kate."

"One good thing that's happened out of

all this is He brought us together," said Kate.

"That is a good thing," choked Mattie.

"Mattie?"

"Yes?"

"What about Sheriff Larson?"

"What about him?" Mattie asked.

"Why haven't you ever married him?" asked Kate.

"I guess I never had the strength ta tell him about my past, and I feel like I'd be cheatin' him."

"Has he asked you?"

"Yeah, he used ta ask me all the time, and now I guess he's resigned to bein' single and to us bein' good friends."

"You know, Mattie, when Jesus comes into your heart, He makes everything new and clean."

"Does He now? I look at this brand-new dress ya wore to the picnic, Kate, and know that after it gets washed, it'll never be as nice and new as it was that first time. So how can He make somethin' old and used, like me, new and clean?"

"I don't know how He does it, Mattie, but I read it in the Bible. It says, 'Therefore if any man be in Christ, he is a new creature: old things are passed away; behold, all things are become new.' "

"Well, Kate, that would be somethin' all right! Maybe I'll do some thinkin' on that, but in the meantime, we'd better get back ta this washin'!"

"Oh, my!" exclaimed Kate. "You're right!"

Both women were quiet as they worked, reflecting on what had been shared. Mattie felt a smoldering fire of shame searing her soul as she pondered on the strange things Kate had told her about getting a clean heart.

Inside Kate, a fountain of joy bubbled up. She knew God was doing a work. She would ask Ben about that church. "Please, Jesus," she prayed, "be changing Mattie's heart. Amen."

CHAPTER 12

A few days later Ben stopped in at Tucker House. Kate happened to be coming in from the henhouse when she saw him ride up. Her heart felt like a giant hammer in her breast. Her emotions were always in a tumult when Ben was around, but today the feelings intensified because she wanted to talk to him about starting a church. She headed toward the house to greet him.

Ben noticed a sparkle in her eyes as she approached. She looked so radiant, so beautiful. He hated to tell her!

"Hello, Ben."

"Hello, Kate."

"Come on in."

"Could we just sit here on the porch a spell, Kate?"

"Sure." Kate saw concern in Ben's expression. "Something wrong?"

"Well, something is troubling me. I hate to worry you about it, but I must tell you."

98

"Go ahead, Ben," Kate urged. A sense of helplessness constricted her throat.

"We had some visitors last night."

"What kind of visitors?"

"Troublesome ones. They rode through our farm shooting holes into the barn."

"Was anyone hurt?"

He nodded sadly. "They killed our dog," he said.

"Oh no!" Kate cried. "I'm so sorry, Ben." Tears welled up in her eyes. She remembered once again the Indian raid of her childhood. "But who would do such a thing?" Terrified, she asked, "I–Indians?"

"There were two riders. We got a glimpse from behind, and they weren't Indians."

"But who then?"

Ben sat still, considering how to tell her. His impulse was to take her in his arms and protect her, but he refrained. As she returned his gaze, she read his expression of concern and then she knew!

"You think it was Tanner?"

"He's the only one I can think of with something against us. From behind it looked like Tanner and Jake. I just got back from talking to the sheriff so he will keep an eye out for Tucker House."

"You think he'd take revenge on me?"

Ben reached over and took her hand for a

moment. "I don't know, Kate, but I'm real fond of you and your family. I don't want to take any chances."

"Oh! This is terrible! I am so ashamed!"

"Please don't blame yourself, Kate. It's not your fault."

"What if he does something else to you, or Luke, or your pa? What he already did is just awful. I'm so sorry, Ben!"

"We're on alert now so don't fret about us. It's you I'm worried about."

"Ben?"

"Yes?"

"C—could we pray?"

"Well, sure, Kate." Ben looked both astonished and very pleased. "Kate, I thought you were a Christian," he said softly.

"Yes, I am. I've known the Lord since I was a little girl. When I first heard you talking about God, I was thrilled. You see, Mattie and the girls aren't Christians. Not yet. They will be someday, though, because I'm praying for them."

Ben leaned forward, elbows resting on his knees, his head turned toward Kate, listening as she explained. A river of warmth flooded over him, washing him with God's love. He did not understand what God was doing just yet, but he recognized His presence.

"Ben?" Kate trembled.

"Yes?"

"Would your pa consider starting a church here at Beaver Creek? The need is so great! I read my Bible, but there are parts I could use some help with . . . parts that need explaining. I'd like to learn hymns, too."

"Haven't you ever gone to church?" he asked tenderly.

"No."

"It's a miracle how God has kept you all these years, Kate, with no church and no one to share with."

"He is faithful. Maybe sometime I'll share some of my experiences with you."

"I'd like that."

There was silence as they sat on the porch, thinking about their Lord. It felt so good for them to share in this way. "I know!" said Ben. "Would you like me to pick you up tomorrow in our buggy and bring you to the farm? You've never been there. You could talk to Pa yourself. I don't know how he can resist you with those big, brown, pleading eyes of yours, but that's not to say that he'll agree to it."

"Oh, yes!"

"Now, let's pray together," suggested Ben. "Would you like to hold my hand while we pray, like we're in agreement?"

"Sure, Ben. That would be nice. I–I've never prayed with anyone before."

Ben took her hand and prayed out loud. "Dear Father, I thank You for bringing Kate into my life. I thank You that she has a hunger for You. I pray that You will make it clear as a bell so Pa can make the right decision about preaching. You know what Kate wants, Lord, but we ask that Your will be done in this matter.

"Lord, I pray for Your protection on Kate and those at Tucker House. We pray for Tanner. May Your grace turn him away from revenge. Please send someone to witness to him in Your name so he can become a Christian. Amen."

"But I didn't get to pray!"

"Okay, go ahead."

"Dear Jesus, I thank You for Your hand guiding me and protecting me. You have so many times in the past that I trust you to continue to do so. Please protect Ben and his family, and help them to know how to deal with Tanner. Lord, You know how Beaver Creek is needing a church. Please help Ben's pa to say yes." At this point she opened her eyes and sneaked a peek at Ben. His eyes were closed, but he was smiling. She continued, "Thank You for bringing the Wheelers to Beaver Creek. Amen."

Ben gave Kate's hand a squeeze.

"Thank you, Ben," she said. "Won't you come inside for awhile?"

"No, I think I'd best be getting home. The sheriff will be by tonight to check the house. Be sure to bolt the door. I'll be by tomorrow about one o'clock."

"Great! Good-bye, Ben."

"Good-bye, Kate."

Kate went inside with the basket of eggs that she had brought an hour before from the henhouse. Mattie said, "I see your friend was visiting," and emphasized the *friend* part. Then she gave Kate a smile and a hug.

Kate sighed. "Yes, but he came to give me some bad news." She told Mattie all that Ben had said and concluded with words of assurance. "The sheriff will check on us. I prayed with Ben, and he is taking me to his farm tomorrow to talk with Mr. Wheeler about preaching." Even though she tried, Kate could not pass on to Mattie the peace that she herself felt inside. Mattie did not know Jesus, the source of the peace.

Mattie felt miserable. She was thinking, *If God wants ta work in my life, now's a good time to start, with all these troubles.*

CHAPTER 13

Kate was dressed and eager for Ben to arrive, though fidgety. She rubbed her sweaty hands on the skirt of her light blue calico dress and arranged the ribbons on her plain blue bonnet. Pacing to the window, she gazed out and then returned to her chair, where she had laid some hand sewing for Mattie.

"Goin' ta the window won't make him come any sooner," Mattie said.

Kate blushed, but then she heard his buggy approaching. "Well, seems like it did after all," she piped up smugly, but with a grin.

"I hope it works out for ya, Kate."

"Thanks, Mattie. Don't wait supper for me; I forgot to ask when I'd be back."

She laid the sewing aside and rushed to the door, giving Ben a warm welcome.

"Well, that's nice. I didn't even have to knock," he teased.

"You did tell me to expect you, remember?" she said blushing.

As they rode along the winding dirt road that led to the Wheelers' place, Kate asked on impulse, "What did you tell your pa about inviting me to the farm?"

Now it was Ben's turn to blush. "Shucks, I was so excited about your idea that I didn't even think about appearances. I just told him I was bringing you over for the afternoon. No wonder he grinned at me that way."

"In what way, Ben?"

"Why, he probably thinks I'm courting you," he said, getting redder by the minute. "I hope that doesn't embarrass you, Kate. I'll set him straight first chance I get."

Kate felt a lump forming in her throat. "Of course," she said numbly just as they approached the farm.

"Well, this is it," Ben said proudly. He pulled the buggy up to the barn and helped Kate down. "I'll unhitch the team, and then I'll show you around."

Kate watched him as he worked. She remembered her first impression of him, how she'd respected him for not embarrassing her with pretty words like Tanner. Yet she found herself longing to hear just such words rolling off his tongue. Sweet as honey they would be coming from Ben. Instead, he said painful things like, "I'll set him straight first chance I get."

"All set," Ben said, bringing Kate out of her reverie.

"Great."

"Over there is the ground we've been clearing," Ben said, pointing. "That's where we'll be planting the corn next spring."

"I can't believe how much you've done in the short time you've been here!"

"I love working the land, Kate. It's what I want to do with my life and is about as natural as breathing to me. Well, here we are." Ben held the door open as Kate went inside.

"Hello, Mrs. Potter."

"Hello, Kate, good to see ya! Would you two be likin' some tea or some coffee?"

"Coffee would be great," Ben said as he walked over to Mrs. Potter and patted her arm affectionately. "Thank you, Mary. Kate, I don't know what we'd do without this lady. She's a wonder. Her sons are fine lads, too, and hard workers!"

Kate was glad it had worked out for them, but she felt a pang of jealousy as she watched her working in Ben's kitchen and wondered what it would be like to cook for Ben and his family. The coffee was soon ready. As they sat and chatted, Kate noticed that everything in the cabin was in perfect order. She wondered if it was always like that, or if it was just because Mrs. Potter had been there that morning. It was, undoubtedly, a bachelor's home; the touch of a woman was missing.

Soon Ben was saying, "Pa's working on the fence along with James and Frank. Let's go and have our talk with him, Kate." Mrs. Potter looked in wonder, and then with understanding. It sounded like a proposal plan to her. Kate and Ben both understood at once.

"Oh, no, Mrs. Potter. It's not what it sounded like," Ben said earnestly.

"Wasn't thinkin' nothin', Ben," she replied smiling. "If it was somethin', I'd be hearin' it sooner or later anyway. Here, take this pitcher of cool water to your pa and the boys." Her eyes crinkled from smiling.

Ben shrugged and said, "Kate?"

She quickly followed Ben out-of-doors. They headed past the barn, where Kate saw a newly turned mound. Ben's gaze rested on it, and then he quickly looked away.

Probably his dog, she thought sadly. Then she spotted Mr. Wheeler and the boys building a rail fence out of timber they had cut to clear the land. Mr. Wheeler dropped the piece he held, rubbed his arm across his brow, and ran his fingers through his thick snowy hair. His eyes were dancing with mischief.

"Howdy," he said.

"Pa." Ben nodded.

"Hello, Mr. Wheeler, James, Frank," said Kate. "You've done so much with your place," she added, turning to Emmett.

"That we have, Miss. Got a long way to go yet, too."

"Here's a drink Mrs. Potter sent for you."

Mr. Wheeler and the boys drank deeply until satisfied. "Mm, that hits the spot. Boys, take a short break. Run in and see if your ma needs anything first. Sure is getting hot these days!"

"Yes, we could use a good rain," Kate said. "Where's Luke?"

"He's clearing the land to the east." Then straight to the point, he added, "Ben doesn't usually ask for the afternoon off so I didn't press him for his reasons. Figured it was something important." He gave Kate a wink.

"Mr. Wheeler," Kate said, "as a matter of fact it is important to me. I'm a Christian and . . ."

"Well, glory be! That's real good news, Kate!" Mr. Wheeler exclaimed.

"Well, yes," she said, stealing a glance at Ben. He nodded his encouragement, and she continued, "But Mattie, Claire, and Annabelle, and lots of other folks around here aren't."

"Sad to hear that," Mr. Wheeler said.

"All I've learned has been straight from the Bible with no one to teach me."

"Nothing wrong with that. The Holy Spirit is the best teacher you could have, Kate."

"Yes, but I have so many questions, and I sure wish there was a church so others could learn about Jesus."

"Hmm, I see." Mr. Wheeler leaned on the fence and scratched his chin.

"Mr. Wheeler, would you consider starting a church in Beaver Creek?" Her eyes searched and pleaded.

"Well now, that certainly wasn't what I was expecting to hear this afternoon." Mr. Wheeler cleared his throat, studied Ben a moment, and then continued. "Can't say it comes as a great surprise though. Two things already happened to prepare me for this question."

"What's that, Pa?" asked Ben.

"First, when we were coming west along the Ohio River, I met a man at camp one night. His name was John Chapman. Appleseed, people called him." He stopped his story to chuckle.

Kate asked, "Appleseed?" while Ben listened. He'd met the man also but didn't know what his pa was going to share.

"Yep. Appleseed. A nice fella. He's planting apple seeds across Ohio and selling seedlings. Actually, he gives half of them away. Got a couple myself. They're planted right over there behind the cabin." He pointed toward the cabin. "Anyway, he's a man of God, and I had a good chat with him that night by the campfire. I'd shared our plans to farm so he knew I wasn't coming west to preach. The next day as we fixed to leave, he gave me those seedlings. He said, 'Plant these, and someday I'll come check on them. When I do, I'll come to your church and hear ya preach.' I guess that was the first word the Lord sent me."

"What was the other, Mr. Wheeler?"

"A dream. It was the night we supped with you at Tucker House. I dreamed I was walking in a field of corn when a wind came from the north and swept me up. It set me down on the edge of the field where sheep fed on a green pasture. They drank water from a brook. A voice said, 'Feed my flock.'

"As I watched the sheep grazing, a lamb came romping through the cornfield. Everywhere he leaped, the corn was trodden and destroyed. 'Go away,' I shouted. 'Get out of my corn.' Then I heard the voice again. It said, 'Feed my flock.' So I allowed the lamb to come across the field and enter the pasture. As he did, other lambs followed. I looked back at the cornfield and all the corn sprung up, unharmed. It was a vivid dream and I knew it held a special meaning. I stored it in my heart."

"Pa! You've been keeping this all inside, and it seemed so right to bring Kate here. I didn't even think about the implications. The Lord must be leading you to do this then."

"It seems so, Son, but we need to have a family meeting and talk it over with Luke. Let us pray about it and talk it over as a family, and then I'll give you my answer, Kate."

"Thank you, Mr. Wheeler." Kate grabbed his hands and pumped them up and down. Tears flowed down her cheeks.

"Don't cry, Kate," Ben said.

"It's just so beautiful how Jesus leads us. He's so good!" she said wiping her tears on her sleeve.

"That He is! That He is!" exclaimed Mr. Wheeler nodding.

"Well, Pa, I'll take Kate home."

"Enjoy yourself, Son; you may not get another day off so easily!" Ben laughed. "Bye, Kate, and thank you for coming today."

"Bye, Mr. Wheeler," Kate shouted.

Later that night three men sat around a small wooden table, heads bowed as the father prayed. "Thank You, God, for sending Your Son, Jesus, to die on the cross so our sins can be forgiven. Guide and direct us as I do what we believe is Your will, feeding the flock here at Beaver Creek. Amen."

CHAPTER 14

Kate wiped her damp brow with the back of her sleeve. Limp hair was twisted into a knot and secured with a white scarf, except for a few unruly strands tickling the nape of her neck. Her old brown dress was frayed and worn through in places, but comfortable and suitable for the day's chores.

It was another hot day, and the windows gaped open in protest. Mercifully, a gentle breeze stirred the curtains while the sweet melody of robins drifted through the open window.

She scrubbed the wooden floor, thinking about the terrible mess the girls had made when they prepared the bread that rose in pans waiting to be baked. They were gone now, at Cooper's General Store with the eggs and visiting their friend, Dorie, whose father owned the store.

When she heard a knock at the door, she plopped the rag into the bucket and dried her hands on her apron as she stood to her feet. "Oh, dear. What a sight I must be!" She tiptoed to the door and pulled it open, trying not to track up the freshly cleaned floor.

"Good morning, Kate."

"Morning, Sheriff Larson!" Kate smiled and motioned toward the wet floor. "I'd invite you in, but the floor's all wet."

"That's all right, Kate. The porch is fine. Is Mattie around?"

"She's out in the garden." Kate nodded.

"Thanks a lot. I'll be heading around the side of the house then." He paused a moment, wondering if he should say what was on his mind, and then continued. "Oh, Kate. I thought you might like to know that Tanner is in Dayton, which means he won't be around for awhile." Buck watched the roses fade from Kate's cheeks as she grew pale.

Kate took a deep breath. "Good," was all she said.

Sheriff Larson turned and left the porch. As he rounded the corner of the house, he spotted Mattie kneeling in the garden and heard her humming sweetly. He sighed, put his hands in his pockets, and headed toward her.

Kate finished her work and carried the

heavy bucket of dirty water onto the porch. It had been a week since she had been to the Wheelers, and she still had not heard from them. It did not seem like Ben and Luke to stay away so long. Just then Annabelle and Claire interrupted her thoughts as they bounded up the porch steps to the door.

"Guess what? Guess what?" exclaimed Annabelle excitedly.

"What?" asked Kate.

"Mr. Cooper says next Saturday there will be a barn raising. Some new folks arrived about a week ago." Annabelle talked so rapidly that Kate had to strain to get all the words. "Folks have already helped them start their cabin, but the barn raising is Saturday. And everybody will be there!"

"Good!" replied Kate. "More new folks. That's wonderful. I'll bake some berry pies."

"Oh, can we help?" asked Claire.

"Sure," said Kate. "I'll teach you how to clean up after yourselves while we're at it!"

"Oh, I knew you had a scolding for us!" said Annabelle, pouting.

"Oh, pooh!" Kate laughed. The girls ran outside, and Kate gazed out the window after them. She noticed Mattie and Buck sitting on the bench under the hickory tree.

Claire popped her head back in and announced, "Ben's here! Ben's here!"

"Oh, no!" Kate said. "What a fright I am!" With that she turned her back to the door, lifted her ragged skirt, and bolted for the stair steps. Her intentions of cleaning up were thwarted when she heard the sound of his voice directly behind her.

"Hello, Kate. Claire let me in."

She stopped abruptly, and her hands flew up to brush back her wild hair. Well, she was caught now and must be hospitable. She shrugged and turned to greet him.

Kate did not miss the look of amusement on Ben's face as he caught sight of her. Slowly he looked her over, from head to toe, taking in her disarrayed hair and ragged gown. She burned with embarrassment. "Come in. Sit down," she said, pointing to a chair and trying to direct his attention away from herself.

"Thanks," Ben said as he sat. He grinned as he reflected on the purpose of his visit. He brought good news and would enjoy letting her drag it out of him.

"Would you like something to drink?" Kate asked. She wished he would not gaze at her with that silly grin. She felt so ill at ease.

"That would be real good, Kate."

She poured him some cold water and sat

down rigidly across the table from him. Ben sensed her frustration and almost refrained from further teasing. But his sense of humor overpowered him. On impulse, he reached over and touched her cheek with his finger. "A smudge," he said smiling.

She felt the color rising up her neck and face. Flustered, she apologized, "I'm sorry. I'm a terrible mess."

"You should see me at the end of the day," he reassured her. "I look like some poor critter that stumbled into a mud hole."

Kate giggled. "Yes, but it's not even the end of the day yet!" As she spoke, she felt her tension slipping away. *Being with Ben is refreshing and comfortable,* she thought, *like coming home after a long, tiring trip.* Then came the question that had been foremost in her mind the last couple of days. She did not waste another moment.

"Ben, does your pa send me an answer yet?"

"Yes." He grinned at her but said no more.

"Yes?" she asked with trepidation.

"Yes, he sends you an answer."

"Well? What is it?" Kate was frustrated at Ben's teasing mood.

"Yes. The answer is yes." He leaned back, tilting his chair, with satisfaction written all over his face as he watched her eyes light up.

"Oh! Oh! I'm so glad." Kate was up and out of her chair in an instant, rushing to hug Ben. However, a few more steps, and she realized what she was about to do. Appalled at her own improper behavior, she tried to stop herself, tripping in the process, falling and landing right in his lap.

Without a second thought, Ben reached out to catch her. He held her in his arms for just an instant but long enough to know in his heart that it was where she belonged. Her feet dangled, not touching the floor, and she grew frantic. She must get up at once! But time stood still for the moment. Kate heard a creak, then a ripping sound, and in a flash she was part of a pile of twisted body and chair parts, intertwined and deposited in a clump on the kitchen floor.

As the dust settled, she found herself staring directly into Ben's big, blue eyes. They were round with astonishment as he wondered what had happened. His eyebrows raised into a frown, and his face was motionless for a very long moment. Then a smile slowly formed, and he was laughing.

She was such a funny sight! Her little white scarf had been knocked off her head, and her hair knot was working loose. The hair hanging down was swinging wildly and eventually settled over the top of her head and down her forehead. Her expression was one of horror.

"What? What happened?" she asked.

"The chair broke," Ben said, grinning as he released her.

"I'm so sorry. How clumsy of me! I guess I was going to hug you, on a whim. That's what I get for living with a bunch of women who always go around hugging each other."

Ben laughed wildly. She looked comical, but listening to her rationalize was even funnier.

"I'm so sorry, Ben. I'm just so happy!" Kate giggled. They laughed and tried to untangle themselves. Kate rubbed her leg. "I think I'll have a few bruises," she said.

"What are you doing?" Annabelle had just entered the house and stopped dead in her tracks. Claire was right on her heels.

"W—we fell," said Kate.

"The chair broke," added Ben.

Annabelle and Claire just stood gaping as Ben and Kate straightened their clothing and struggled to their feet. Ben slowly bent over and picked up some broken pieces of the chair.

"Looks like I'll have an excuse to come

over now," he said. "I–I mean, I'll need to fix that chair for you."

"You can come anytime, Ben," piped up Claire. "Better make that chair stronger next time."

Ben smiled and started to answer, but Kate interrupted him. Remembering the reason for her excitement, she exclaimed, "Ben, where will we meet, and when will we start?"

"Pa wondered if we could use the schoolhouse. Pa will inquire about it. If we can use it, we can spread the word at the barn raising Saturday. Pa thought you could help with that part."

Kate nodded in agreement, and Ben continued, "I would have been over sooner, but I've been at Mary's, fixing up things. James and Frank are pretty young to be keeping up a place."

"You have? That's so thoughtful of you."

"Mary doesn't seem to be the type to take over the farm, either. She's a great lady, strong on the inside, if not on the outside."

"I'm so glad you can help each other."

"That's what friends do, Kate." She wondered if he was stressing the word *friends* for her sake. "Well, I'd better get into town for my supplies and back to the farm before Pa sends Luke looking for me." He looked fondly at Kate.

"Thanks so much for stopping by, Ben. I have so much to look forward to now."

Ben picked up the pieces of chair and asked, "Mind if I take these with me? It'll be easier to fix at home." He winked and walked out the door.

As Ben rode away, he shook his head and laughed. Kate was full of surprises. Then his thoughts sobered as he realized he was falling in love with this girl, another man's girl. *But it felt so right when she was in my arms,* he moaned.

CHAPTER 15

Folks from all around Beaver Creek gave a hearty welcome to their new neighbors with a barn raising. The men fashioned temporary tables out of wood, and the women loaded them with the sumptuous foods prepared all morning for the noonday meal. Big iron kettles bubbled with beans and hominy. Platters of meat stacked high, golden cornbread, sweet rice pudding, and tempting pies sent their aromas wafting through the summer air.

Kate held a fat, squirmy baby boy. His name was Joey, and he belonged to the new family, the Morgans. The children played a game of Snap the Whip; the heat did not seem to bother them. Claire found friends that she had not seen since Independence Day. Sammy Hawkes eagerly showed the girls his arrowhead collection. He dug in the pockets of his patched and faded overalls to display his many treasures. The girls envisioned painted Indians with bow and arrow, spotted ponies, and tall tepees, as Sammy stuttered his knowledge on the subject. They did not mind his stuttering; he was a hero.

Kate turned to face the barn. The walls were already up. The men used forked poles to raise the center ridgepole higher. She spotted Ben and Luke hauling lumber to the work site, carrying it across their shoulders.

Their muscles bulged through their cotton shirts, rolled up at the sleeves. Sweat dripped down their faces. Yet they looked like they enjoyed the companionship of the other men.

Just then Kate jolted, startled by a sudden cracking noise, like a deer's antlers crashing through a thicket, only louder. Ben and Luke dropped their lumber and raced toward the barn. Kate saw a part of the structure give way. Men catapulted off the top of the barn wall and plummeted to the ground, much like hot cinders spurting skyward out of a burning fire, then extinguishing and falling to the earth. It was a terrible sight. Kate gasped and clung tightly to little Joey.

Dan Whitfield and Jess Bennett rushed to the scene and anxiously bent over Graham

Malone, the town doctor, who seemed to be the worst. He moaned and tried to speak. Emmett Wheeler and Sheriff Larson helped those who had fallen. They carefully aided them to their feet, inspecting their bodies for injury. It was soon evident that only the doctor was badly hurt. Mack Tillson, the blacksmith, landed on his side and had a large scrape. Blood seeped through his shirt, but he motioned the others away, insisting that he was all right. As he rose, he limped stiffly, trying to work out the kinks.

Bennett said, "Doc's leg is badly fractured. It's bleeding, and the bone is exposed."

"We need to make a tourniquet fast," ordered Whitfield.

The doctor's wife ran to his side and placed her hand tenderly on his forehead. Sarah Morgan piped up, "I'll run to the house and be right back with some clean rags." Her skirts flew as she sped past Kate.

"Ma–ma," Joey cried as he got a glimpse of Sarah rushing by. Kate reached up and tenderly patted Joey's cheek, so soft and smooth. She reassured him that his ma would be right back. Kate heard the sound of horses fast approaching and, wondering who it could be at such a time, looked toward the road. To her horror, it was three dark-skinned Indian braves. Kate felt her body tense, frigid with fright. Frozen to the spot, she looked frantically toward the barn, struggling with an intense desire to run to safety. There she saw Ben, standing straight and tall, and drew enough strength from his unruffled composure to whisper soft words of assurance to little Joey.

Sheriff Larson and Carl Hawkes hurried over to the Indians, who were still mounted on their horses. Carl used hand signals and arm motions to communicate with them. Sammy, followed close by Claire, ran breathlessly and stopped to stand beside his father. Kate's heart stopped as she heard Mattie call out sharply, "Claire!"

Mr. Hawkes looked at the children and raised his arm out beside him, motioning for them to remain quiet and still. Then he continued to communicate with the Indian braves. At last he said loudly, "These Wyandot Indians, Little Bear and two braves, are headed to the reservation at Sandusky. They mean no harm. They heard the commotion. Bein' curious, they came to investigate and think they can help. The one called Little Bear seems to know about medicines."

There was muttering along with bits of arguing, and then Bennett said, "No! They're heathens. He's probably a witch doctor."

"Are you going to set the doctor's leg then?" asked Sheriff Larson.

"W–well no, but surely there is someone who can . . . besides these savages. How can we trust them?" argued Bennett.

When Sarah returned with the cloth, she stopped in her tracks. The sheriff nodded, and the Wyandots dismounted off their horses and followed him to the group of men surrounding the doctor. Sarah stepped forward and cautiously handed the cloth to the sheriff, who in turn gave it to Little Bear. Bennett angrily backed away, watching suspiciously as the Indians kneeled down and worked over the doctor.

The doctor moaned again and passed out as Little Bear wound the cloth tightly above the fractured part of the doctor's leg. Little Bear quickly and skillfully set the leg. One of the other Indians handed him a small deerskin pouch, and he removed a bad-smelling ointment, which he plastered generously over the doctor's leg. Then he loosened the tourniquet and bound the leg with more of the cloth that Sarah had provided. Soon the Indians were finished. Bennett quickly moved forward and resumed caring for the doctor. He and Whitfield carried the doctor inside the cabin.

Joe Morgan placed his arm around his

wife Sarah and said with a booming voice, "It's almost noon. I thank you folks for all your help today. Perhaps we should call it a day . . . since this accident. But the women worked hard, cooking all morning, and we're all hungry, so let's stop now and eat while we decide what should be done."

Emmett Wheeler said, "I think we should share our lunch with Little Bear and his braves."

There was silence followed by some grumbling, and then Carl Hawkes began with more hand motions. The Wyandots nodded and followed him and the others down to the springhouse to clean up with the buckets of cool water that waited there. They lined up under the oak trees and relaxed as they helped themselves to heaping plates of food.

"Cute little fellow," a voice said over Kate's shoulder. She turned to see Luke standing beside her.

"Luke! Yes, he's a cute little rascal," she said, giving him a tickle. Just then Annabelle appeared at her side.

"Can I hold him, Kate?"

"Sure! Here he is. Keep your eye on him every minute now," she warned as she handed the precious little bundle to Annabelle. She turned to Luke and said, "Sit down, Luke, and rest while you can."

"Sounds good, but only if you'll join me." He eased himself down onto the soft, damp grass while balancing his plate on his knees.

Luke saw the troubled look on Kate's face. He followed her gaze and saw Ben talking to Melanie Whitfield. "Are you all right, Kate?" he asked. "You're looking mighty pale."

"It's just the Indians. They frighten me," she said. Kate did not realize that part of her uneasiness stemmed from the scene taking place between Ben and Melanie. Luke, however, surmised as much.

Across the way, Melanie was detaining Ben. "I'm so frightened of those savages," she whined, clutching his arm.

"Why, you've nothing to be frightened of. There are only three Indians among all of us. I'm sure they won't start trouble."

"You're right, but I'd feel much better if you'd just stay here with me." She clung to his arm.

"As a matter of fact, I was on my way to see what they are up to. Come on, Melanie. Be brave and come with me?" he coaxed.

"Well, I don't know. All right then, but stay right by my side." She clutched his arm tighter.

Ben chuckled as they strolled over to join those gathered around the red-skinned

Wyandots. He was curious and wanted to get a closer look at the Indians.

They joined a small circle of children, including Sammy and Claire, who sat on the grass about ten feet away from the braves. Ben saw Indians on their trip west, but nevertheless, he was awed each time anew. He settled down with his plate, able to observe without being noticed because Melanie was close at his side. He watched as Mr. Hawkes carried on a conversation with the natives, consisting of words accompanied by many hand movements.

Two of the Indians wore deerskin loincloths with pouches tied at their waists, embroidered with dyed moose hair. Little Bear had on a deerskin coat as well, trimmed at the cuff and collar with dyed porcupine quills. They wore beads made of shells, and their moccasins were deerskin dyed black and decorated with embroidery.

Sammy poked Ben, and he bent his head down to listen as Sammy whispered, stammering into his ear. "W–why i–is o–one d–different?"

Ben whispered back, "I was wondering the same thing. I'll bet your dad will know. Seems like he's getting a lot of information out of them."

Claire giggled and pointed. "Look at their

funny hats!"

"Shh!" Melanie scolded.

"They can't understand me!" she said in a pouty voice.

They wore silly-looking hats made out of beaver skin and adorned with colorful feathers.

Across the yard, Luke finished eating. Kate took his plate and headed toward the tables where the other women stood to serve. Throughout the morning, Kate and the Wheelers spread the word about starting church meetings. There had been a lot of interest, and Kate had held high hopes until just now. As she walked past a group of men, she overheard Bennett saying to Whitfield, "If this is the kind of doin's that comes from having a preacher among us, I ain't so sure I'm for it. I'd just as soon kill them savages as to look at them."

Kate's heart sank in confusion. Whenever she saw Indians, she remembered the massacre at Big Bottom. The Wheelers showed compassion to the savages. These Indians actually helped them! Could she ever forgive? No, she did not think so! She was learning something new about herself. She realized that her heart was filled with hatred as well as fear.

When the meal was finished, the Indians

departed unceremoniously. Soon after, the Bennetts followed the Malone wagon to see them home safely. Doc Malone's wife drove the team. She could best care for him now, with the bone set and the bleeding stopped. The other men decided to continue working on the barn.

About an hour before dark, just as the men finished thatching the roof with bark, lightning flashed, followed by a loud clap of thunder. They had worked hard and steady, determined to get the barn up before the rain fell. Contrary to Kate's fears, no confrontations developed after the Indians left. The men stuck together, letting their resentments, frustrations, and hatred simmer quietly inside, where God looks upon the heart.

Then the rain fell in heavy torrents with more lightning and thunder. The horses grew nervous. Men scurried off the barn and searched for their families. It was time to quit even though the barn was not quite finished. Most of the women had already loaded the wagons, expecting to leave quickly. Some of the women and children took cover in the cabin at the onset of the cloudburst while a few of the children remained outside, running wildly and playing in the rain. Soon the confusion was over, and most of the families headed home.

The dirt road quickly became a ribbon of sticky mud, and wagons made ruts in the road, getting stuck in the potholes. Friends stopped to help each other as needed. Everyone got soaked.

"Guess we should have given up an hour ago," Sheriff Larson said to Mattie as they rode along. "We hoped it would hold off awhile yet."

Claire, Annabelle, and Kate huddled together in the back of the wagon bed with a blanket draped over their heads. "This is fun," exclaimed Claire. "This was the best day I ever had."

"Yes!" agreed Annabelle. "It was a good day . . . and so exciting with the Indians and everything. Don't you think so, Kate?"

"I could do without this rain," admitted Kate, "and without the Indians, too."

"Pooh! I wasn't scared a bit!" piped up Claire. Just then a gush of water rushed under the blanket and onto the back of Claire's neck. "Oooh!" she screamed. Then Annabelle got wet and let out a shriek.

"We're almost there, gals. Just hold on a little longer!" yelled the sheriff from the front of the wagon. "Mattie, I'm so sorry. You doing all right?"

Mattie was drenched through and through

and starting to chill, but her smile was as warm as a summer's sun when she answered him.

Just then a wild thought entered Kate's mind. *I wonder where those Indians are right now and if they're getting soaked, too?* And again she asked herself, *Will I ever forgive them?*

CHAPTER 16

After a week of rain and some exhausting days spent cleaning the schoolhouse that had been boarded up for summer, Sunday finally arrived. Ben observed the calm sky with a sigh of gratitude. "Do you reckon God arranged it special for the sun to shine over Beaver Creek's first church meeting, Luke?"

"It sure seems like it," Luke replied cheerfully. As the brothers did chores, they talked. "I'm so glad Father's preaching again," Luke said.

"Me, too; it feels so right."

"Ben? You got special feelings for Kate?"

"W–what?" The question startled Ben.

Luke repeated the question. Still, Ben did not answer. "She really lights up when you come around. I think she's sweet on you."

"Naw, she can't be; she's got a beau already," Ben said sullenly.

"Nonsense! You know Tanner's a scoundrel."

"No, not Tanner . . . someone else."

"What makes you so sure?"

"She said so. I overheard her praying." Ben's face flushed from the memory of it.

"Praying?"

"Yeah. She said that he has a heart as big as all outdoors and he is handsome and strong. She said he's a Christian. . . . She even dreams about him."

"Well, I don't know about the handsome part," Luke teased.

"What?"

"It's as plain as that freckled nose on your face!" Luke grinned at the irony of the situation.

"What do you mean?" Ben demanded.

"It sounds to me like she described you."

"Me?" His mind whirled, reliving that scene again like so many times before. *Could it be?* he wondered.

"Did you ever see her with another fella?" Luke asked.

"Well, no . . . but I can't believe it. You really think so? All this time I've been thinking . . ."

"She acted upset when you sat with Melanie at the barn raising," Luke confided. He reached up and grabbed Ben's hat, giving it a tug. "If I were in your shoes, Brother, I'd go calling."

Ben considered the possibility until Luke brought his head back down out of the clouds. "We better hurry up and finish chores. It's Sunday, remember?"

"Do I!" Ben grinned.

Meanwhile, Sheriff Larson arrived at Tucker House to pick up the ladies for church. "Mattie, I'd like you to meet my nephew, Thaddeas Larson. He's my brother's boy all the way from Boston. He's going to stay with me a spell and try out the West."

"My pleasure," said Thaddeas.

Kate stared foolishly. This was a gentleman dressed in fine Boston clothes. He was built short and sturdy with black, wavy hair and dark, warm eyes.

After the introductions they were on their way in Sheriff Larson's wagon. At the schoolhouse Carl Hawkes and his family pulled up, and Miss Forrester, the school mistress, came from across the meadow.

Inside, Kate waved to the Coopers and stopped to talk to Dr. Malone and his family. He walked with a crutch.

Sheriff Larson followed Mattie to an empty bench. Claire and Annabelle sat beside them. Thaddeas motioned for Kate to go ahead then positioned himself at her side, and they all squeezed together to make room. Kate continued to look around. Not everyone was there, but enough families came to make it all worthwhile. Her face glowed with happiness. Then she spied Ben and Luke sitting in the front row, and she smiled and waved her handkerchief.

Ben returned her smile, noticing how radiant she looked. Then he saw the stranger at her side. Cut to the quick, he took it all in. The stranger definitely came from the East. *It's him, the man of her prayers.* He turned to Luke in panic and saw his own hurt mirrored in his brother's eyes.

But Luke whispered, "Don't give up, Ben."

Heads bowed as their father prayed, "Lord, we give You thanks for allowing us to gather and worship You!" Amens echoed throughout the room.

Kate was surprised as Sarah Morgan led them in singing "The Old Rugged Cross." Her voice was melodious, sweet and high, and the singing was like a taste of heaven to Kate and the others who had waited so long for this moment.

Mr. Wheeler, henceforth called Rev. Wheeler, preached on forgiveness.

Kate fought to gain control of her emotions. Her conscience awoke to truth. She had bitterness in her heart toward Tanner, toward the Indians.

Thaddeas whispered to Kate, pointing behind the Reverend where a skunk boldly pranced across the front of the room.

He grabbed Kate's hand, and they joined a throng of folks squeezing out the back.

Somehow everyone escaped without offending the intruder. As Rev. Wheeler stepped outside he said, "Thank You, Lord, for a sunny day where we can finish worshiping You in this glorious setting fashioned by Your own hands. If we can *forgive* the little creature, we can continue." There was laughter, and he wrapped up his sermon.

When the meeting was over, Sheriff Larson stole Thaddeas away and introduced him to his friends. Luke elbowed his brother. "Go now. See how the land lies." He gave Ben a little push.

He stumbled, shot Luke a disgruntled look, then shuffled forward.

"Ben! It was just like I imagined it would be! It was just glorious . . . even with the skunk."

Her excitement and laughter soon soothed his jitters. "Yes, it was a funny sight, everyone in their Sunday best acting like a bunch of wildcats."

"Your pa was wonderful. He just let the skunk keep the schoolhouse and continued outside. His words were profound."

"It must have been the Lord speaking to you, Kate. Pa's words aren't nothing special. I hear them every day. No harm intended," he added as he grinned. Then the words slipped out without warning. "You look beautiful today, Kate."

Kate blushed. "Thank you," she said softly.

"I'd like you to meet my nephew, Thaddeas," interrupted Sheriff Larson.

Ben's face burned red with anger. Overwhelmed with a strong desire to give the newcomer a swift kick in the pants, instead he shook Thaddeas's hand. Kate gave Ben her sweetest smile and said, "I'm going to go thank your pa, Ben."

"Rev. Wheeler, I'd like to know more about forgiveness." Then with her small white hand in his big rough one, Kate released the bitterness and hatred that had robbed her peace.

CHAPTER 17

The sun peeked through black clouds that threatened rain again as Kate strolled along the creek with Annabelle and Claire. Its brown, muddy waters rushed high and swift with recent rains. Claire and Annabelle explored the banks, probing and poking under rocks and pebbles at the water's edge with hickory branches that also served as walking sticks.

Claire asked, "Do you suppose the creek could run over and drown folks?"

"I suppose it could, although it doesn't seem likely. But I don't remember it this high before," Kate replied.

"Maybe the beavers have it dammed," Annabelle suggested.

"That's very likely," Kate replied. "You girls about ready to head back?"

"Oh, Kate, do we have to?" Annabelle moaned.

"Look! Look!" screamed Claire pointing. "A snake!"

"Oh! Let's watch him," yelled Annabelle.

"Let him alone, girls," Kate warned as she motioned them to her side.

"Aw, shucks!" Annabelle obeyed but gave the ground a sound kick with her tiny foot.

Moments later, breathless from climbing, they topped the muddy slope. As they approached home, Kate noticed a familiar black stallion tied. Curious, she halted on the edge of the porch, and there stood Tanner! Kate felt the pounding of blood in her temples, followed by a sudden weakness. The three girls stood still, and Tanner spoke. "Kate, could we talk?"

Flustered, Kate considered a moment. Then she said, "Girls, run in the house and tell Mattie that Tanner is here, and I'm talking to him outside."

The girls ran into the house, both talking at once, and relayed Kate's message. Mattie scurried to the kitchen and poked her nose out the window. She could see them, all right, on the bench under the tree! She promptly found some chores to do in the kitchen, keeping her eyes glued to the window.

"You're looking better than you did the last time I saw you," Kate said pertly.

"I'm sorry about that," he said with a sheepish grin. "Were you jealous, Kate?"

"I certainly was not!" she replied angrily.

"Kate, the reason I acted so foolishly was I had too much liquor," he blurted. "I was the jealous one. Please," he pleaded, "give me another chance!"

"I can't."

"Why?"

"Tanner, there are two reasons. First, I don't trust you."

"Aw, Kate, I made a mistake. It'll never happen again." Looking into his heartsick, blue eyes, she was sorely tempted to believe him.

"Go on," he said.

"The other reason is, I love someone else."

Anger raised its ugly head instantaneously, and Tanner shouted, "Wheeler! It's Wheeler, isn't it? Why, I'll fix his wagon!"

"Tanner, please."

His body was rigid, and his voice hard and low. "Kate, a man has a right to be angry when the woman he loves wants another man."

"Don't you see? There is nothing you can do to make me love you . . . if I don't. Harming Ben won't change my mind," she tried to reason.

"But if I can't have you, it would sure

make me feel a lot better," he cried.

"Did it? Did it make you feel better when you shot up his farm?"

He looked at her, startled. "Yeah! Yeah, it did!" he shouted.

A tear rolled down Kate's cheek. "Don't you see that it will only make you more miserable if you continue this way? It takes a man to accept things that he can't change . . . to be strong, and move on. That's the kind of man I can respect."

"You think folks don't respect me?"

"Tanner, what about that girl in Dayton?"

"What? What girl?"

"The one you always go to see."

"You don't know nothing, Kate. She ain't respectable, not the marrying kind. That's not why I go to see her."

"I see. Listen to me. You have so much in your favor. You're handsome and smart and charming, downright dazzling. Don't throw it away. Think about your future." Another tear rolled down her cheek. "I really care what happens to you, Tanner."

Tanner's jaw was firmly set, his face hard as flint, and Kate could not read his thoughts. "Thanks for seeing me, Kate," he said simply. He stood up, then reached over and gently wiped her tears away. As he felt the wetness on his hand, he stuffed his fist into his pocket, turned, and walked away.

Kate watched him ride away, and as soon as he was gone, she wept. Mattie was out, posthaste, and at Kate's side. "What did he say? What happened?" She handed Kate a handkerchief and waited.

"Oh, Mattie, I don't know. I just don't know."

CHAPTER 18

The long, sultry days of August were jam-packed. Mattie's regular sewing customers placed orders for school clothes. Tucker House became a stockpile of dry goods. There were bolts and bolts of colorful calico prints and cottons, threads, and beautiful laces. Mattie savored each piece of fabric, mixing and matching, designing and cutting. She sewed the little girls' dresses with delight and chatted with their customers. Tucker House was alive with all the latest bits of news and gossip.

With Mattie busy at the needle, Kate and her sisters did the canning and harvesting of the garden's abundant crops. Today they canned tomatoes — a gourmet crop, new in the Ohio Valley. They stewed some of the tomatoes and made juice also. Annabelle and Claire picked and washed the large red, ripe tomatoes. Kate plopped them into a huge kettle with a little water from the springhouse. They bubbled and cooked until mushy for the stewed variety. For the juice, she cooked them longer, smashing and stirring them vigorously with a wooden spoon. Annabelle and Claire washed the jars and filled them with the juicy red fruit.

As they cleaned up from their labors, Kate suggested that they make cold sandwiches and entice Mattie to a picnic lunch. Annabelle eagerly sliced the bread while Claire headed out to the springhouse for a jug of milk and the meat. Kate added greens from the garden and large juicy slices of tomato to the sandwiches.

They spread their blanket on the ground where the grass was soft. The breeze felt cool on Kate's wet face. She wiped her forehead with her arm and rubbed the back of her neck. "Oh, this is much better. I didn't even realize there was a breeze today!" she said.

"You girls want to take the eggs in to Cooper's General Store?" Mattie asked. The girls were always eager to abandon their chores around the house and take the short walk into Beaver Creek, especially to see Dorie.

An hour later, the girls left for town while Mattie was in the house preoccupied with her sewing. Kate decided to clean up at the springhouse since the kitchen was sticky and hot. She washed her long, black hair and then relaxed under the hickory tree. It dried quickly. Reluctantly, she headed indoors.

She changed into fresh clothes, humming as she picked up a dress to hem and joined Mattie in the sitting room. The low tones of male voices floated through the open windows, and Mattie hastened to the door to welcome the visitors. It was Sheriff Larson and Thaddeas.

"Come on in," Mattie welcomed them.

Buck declined the invitation, saying, "We just stopped in to get your permission to do some fishing behind the house. I plan to show Thaddeas one of the real pleasures of life!"

"Why, of course! Go right ahead; enjoy yourselves," Mattie replied.

"Smells good in here," Thaddeas said as the aroma tempted him.

"We canned tomatoes this morning." Kate was pleased that someone appreciated her labors.

"If you care to share your catch, you could join us for supper," Mattie suggested.

"That would be great!" the sheriff said eagerly. "We'd better get to it then. We'll be back with plenty."

"Enjoy yourselves," Mattie called as they

left. She turned to Kate. "Maybe you could bake one of your famous berry pies for supper tonight."

Kate looked at Mattie helplessly. "I suppose so. I was all settled in for a cool afternoon of stitching."

"I know," Mattie said, "but we should be hospitable."

Kate laid down the dress and headed to the kitchen, taking her apron from a peg on the wall. *Life keeps going in circles,* she thought. *You end up doing the same things over and over.* A smile formed on her face and she shrugged. *Friends make it worthwhile.* Then it faded. *Wish it was Ben coming for supper.*

Pies cooled under the window, and tossed greens were mixed with cream. Mattie tucked her sewing away and hummed as she dusted with an old cloth. Annabelle and Claire played marbles in the sitting room.

As Kate scanned the kitchen to see if she had forgotten anything, she heard the men coming. They carried a pail. Kate ran to the door and exclaimed, "Wonderful! You caught all those?"

"Yes, the tempting offer inspired us. Actually, Thaddeas was an able pupil." Buck patted his nephew on the back.

"The credit goes to Uncle Buck, an incredible teacher," Thaddeas replied.

"I'm sure you're both to be thanked. Now I'll take those, and you can clean up at the springhouse." Kate took the pail from the sheriff.

When they returned, Claire showed them to the sitting room, and they relaxed a spell and watched the girls play marbles. They could smell the fish frying, and their mouths watered by the time Mattie called them to supper.

"Fresh trout! It is so delicious! Thank ya so much," Mattie said. "We don't get it often enough."

"You need to let me go fishing," Claire piped up. "All I need is the right equipment. Ben showed me how."

"Well, Claire, I didn't know you liked to fish. We should have taken you with us," the sheriff said with surprise.

"How do you like this country life compared ta Boston, Thaddeas?" asked Mattie.

"I love it! It surpasses my expectations. I hope to find work and settle here permanently."

"Good." Mattie nodded.

"What kind of work?" asked Kate.

"I trained in business, and someday I'd

like to set up a shop. I don't know much about farming. I'd settle for anything in the meantime."

"Something will show up in town. You'll find yourself a spot," Buck said with assurance.

"That was delicious." Thaddeas thanked his hosts when the meal was finished.

The sheriff offered, "Why don't you take Thaddeas and show him your place, Kate. I'll help Mattie with the dishes. She tells me you've been in the kitchen all day."

"Thank you," Kate replied, "I'd like that."

After they had walked a bit, Kate explained the use of the many buildings, amazed at his ignorance of pioneer life. Then they settled on the porch for a chat. "I wonder if anyone got rid of the skunk in the schoolhouse." Thaddeas chuckled.

"I hope so."

"Could be a real stinky job," Thaddeas continued.

Kate laughed. "Most definitely." Then she grew serious and asked, "Have you gone to church before, back East, I mean?"

"Yes, all my life. It's a lot different there though."

"Really? How?"

"It's the folks who are different. In the East everybody is busy, not as caring and friendly. They seem to forget the meaning of being a Christian later in the week. The singing is good but more formal with a choir and everything."

"Last week was the first time I ever went to church."

"No! I thought sure you were a Christian, Kate."

"Oh, I am. I have been since I was a little girl, and you are, too, I can tell. I like that."

"I do, too, Kate," he said sincerely, "and I like the folks here in the valley. I like them a lot."

CHAPTER 19

Ben resolved that the only road to travel was the straight one — to win Kate's heart he must be direct and honest, let her know he cared.

"Whoa! You ungrateful cow, stand still now!" Ben hollered as he shoved the pail to the proper spot with a kick of his boot while planning the day's tactics.

I could ask her to go for a ride this afternoon, or I could mention that I might stop in for awhile. Hmm, I hope she's not tied up with old Thaddeas.

"Ben, I'm all through here. Do you need any help?" Luke called to his brother through the open barn door.

"No, I'm nearly finished. Thanks though."

The schoolhouse stood basking in the sunshine, its doors flung open to welcome the families. Ben took his place in the front and scanned the room.

The Whitfields were new this week, and

Melanie kept an eye on Ben, reliving in her imagination the times they shared together. Dr. Malone limped in with his family. Mary Potter and her sons found a seat beside the Whitfields. They blocked Melanie's view of Ben, and she squirmed in her seat.

Finally, he spotted the ladies from Tucker House. Ben watched them occupy an empty bench, moving all the way toward the wall. He noted anxiously that a good portion of their bench was vacant and sighed with relief when Mack Tillson, the blacksmith, sat beside them.

What! Ben took a second look. *It's Tanner and his friend Jake. Oh, I hope they're not going to make trouble for Pa,* he fretted as he gave Luke a poke. Ben looked at his pa. The Reverend's head was bent, and Ben thought he must be praying for the congregation.

The service started with singing, and the folks who did not know the songs the previous week started to pick up the tunes. Bursting with joy, Kate sang along with all her heart.

Rev. Wheeler told the folks the sweet story of salvation.

Shivers raced up and down Kate's spine. She twisted the handkerchief on her lap. The reality of Jesus' sacrifice overwhelmed her, and she bowed her head to thank Him.

When Tanner stood to his feet, Kate noticed him for the first time and gasped. Tanner made his way, stumbling, to the front while Jake went out the back door.

"I'd like to be forgiven, to tell Jesus I'm sorry. Would He accept me?" Tanner asked. "I want to change my ways."

Tanner knelt, and the Reverend fervently prayed over him. Eyes grew wet throughout the congregation as Tanner experienced release from a life of sin and exchanged his tattered grave clothes for the clean robe of righteousness.

Tanner took a seat on the front bench while Rev. Wheeler faced the people. He raised his arm toward heaven. "There is joy and celebrating in heaven when one lost lamb is saved. Praise God!" He placed his hand on Tanner's shoulder for a moment, patted his back, and then turned toward the assembly. "I have something else very special to share with you folks." He lingered, savoring the moment. "There's going to be a wedding! Mary Potter and I are going to wed as soon as the circuit preacher comes around. You may now welcome our new brother in the Lord, Tanner Matthews, and congratulate my pretty bride-to-be."

Once people were outside, tongues started

wagging with excitement. Everyone was congratulating and backslapping the preacher.

Kate stood among a circle of friends when Tanner appeared. "I'm so happy for you," she said blinking back a tear.

"Aw, you're always crying, Kate . . . every time I'm around."

"That's because I care about you. I told you that before," she said.

He treasured her words in his heart.

"Welcome to the family." Ben held out his hand, and Tanner gripped it firmly.

"Ben? Can I ask you something?"

"Sure, Tanner."

"Why didn't you fight back the night we had our scrap?"

Ben grinned. "The truth is I was aching to."

"Why didn't you?" Tanner probed.

"Because my heart's set to follow Jesus. Let me show you." He thumbed through his Bible until he found Romans 12:18–19. "Here it is, 'If it be possible, as much as lieth in you, live peaceably with all men. Dearly beloved, avenge not yourselves, but rather give place unto wrath: for it is written, Vengeance is mine; I will repay, saith the Lord.' "

"I want to live a decent life, to change,

but I don't know if I can. I'll have to get me a Bible."

"Here, take mine. I have another one at home."

Tanner was overcome with emotion. "Thanks, mighty good of you," he mumbled. He felt a firm grip on his shoulder and turned. It was Luke.

"God bless you," he said.

"He already has." Tanner scanned the groups scattered about the school yard. "I guess my friend Jake took off. I sure wish he could experience this."

Luke nodded. "Come on, let's walk a bit and talk about it. There are a few things we can do for him."

They left Ben and Kate standing alone. Glancing around, Ben caught Thaddeas looking their way. *Better move quick,* he thought. "Kate," he asked, "are you busy this afternoon?"

"Why no, Ben. I don't have anything planned," she said.

"Would you mind if I stopped over for a bit?" He did not realize he was digging a deep rut with his foot.

Kate noticed and thought that something must be troubling him. *Maybe he wants to talk about his pa and Mary getting married,* she thought. "I'd love to have you stop in. You know that, Ben," she said warmly. Then she added, "You can tell me all about your pa and Mary."

"Melanie, my dear, you look so pale!" Mrs. Whitfield said with alarm.

"Mama, did you ever see such a tease? First, she toyed with poor Mr. Matthews, and when he walked away from her, she went straightway to entrap Ben. Let me tell you, Ben's no fool. I'm sure he must be nearly bored to death. I must go rescue him. Ben, oh Ben!"

CHAPTER 20

Ben pushed his food around on his plate with his fork. He could have been chewing on paperboard from Green's Mill for all he cared. Mary Potter had lovingly prepared the meal, and the food was not bad; Ben was just too anxious to enjoy it. Instead he rehearsed what he would say to Kate. *Kate, could I come courting?* or *Kate, you're very special, and I'd like to come calling.*

The Reverend asked him to take Mary and her sons home since he planned to go in that direction. Ben agreed, and now he was biding his time while the meal dragged on and on.

Finally, Mary cleared the table and heated the water in a big black kettle to wash the dirty dishes.

And it was two hours later when they were on their way to the Potter place. Summer's charm captivated Mary. To her right a meadow displayed tall green grasses and a kaleidoscope of wildflowers. To her left passed a lush forest, thick and green, where without warning a doe burst out of a small thicket and dashed wildly in front of the team of horses, then vanished into the forest. It took Ben by surprise, and the horses bolted. The wagon slipped off the edge of the road, careened, and veered into a rut, scraping and bumping wildly behind the horses until it bounced back onto the road.

"Whoa! Whoa!" Ben said as he pulled tightly on the reins. The wagon slowed to a halt and settled in a crazy tilted position. "Just what I was afraid of," Ben said. "We broke a wheel." Disappointed and discouraged from this course of events, he studied what to do. "Will you be all right if I take the team on to your place and come back with your wagon to get you?"

"We'll be fine," Mary assured him. "Take your time, Ben."

"Boys, stay with your ma now, and make sure no harm comes to her!"

"Sure," James and Frank chimed.

Ben unhitched the team and mounted one of his horses bareback, leading the other. The wind whipped under his hat, gently rumpling his hair in disarray, and pushed hard against his shoulders as he rode toward the Potters' place.

Meanwhile back at Tucker House, Kate went to the door, expecting to see Ben. "Hello!" she said cheerfully. Then, "Thaddeas," she added in surprise.

"Good afternoon, Kate," Thaddeas said in his cheerful voice.

"Come in," Kate said.

"Thank you. I was wondering if Claire would like to go fishing?"

"Yes!" cried Claire, who overheard the question. "May I, Mattie?" she begged.

"Of course, that's mighty kind of ya ta be invitin' her, Thaddeas."

"My pleasure," he said sincerely. "Would Annabelle like to come along?"

Annabelle heartily agreed.

Then Thaddeas added, "Kate, would you like to join us, too?"

Kate was tempted but declined. "No, not this time, but thank you."

Thaddeas nodded and headed outside to retrieve the fishing pole propped against a tree. A giggling pair of girls followed him.

"You should have gone along, Kate," Mattie said.

"Ben said he was dropping by this afternoon."

"Oh, I see!" Mattie said. "I see, indeed."

Two hours passed. Thaddeas returned with two fatigued but beaming girls and a pail full of cleaned but smelly fish, presented like an offering, plunked down on the porch by Kate's feet. Kate had walked out onto the porch to scan the roadway when the smiling, smelly little group descended upon her.

"What a catch!" she exclaimed. "Are you sure you are a beginner at this, Thaddeas?"

"I caught most of them," Claire piped up, out of breath.

"You did not!" Annabelle shouted.

"Well, I caught three of them, and big ones, too!" Claire said loudly and firmly.

"Yes, you sure did, Peach," Thaddeas said.

They all looked up when a dusty cloud appeared. As it settled, Ben emerged. He pulled his horse, Pepper, to a halt and slid off his back. He straightened his hat, brushed the dust off his clothes, and stomped about a bit before he noticed, embarrassingly, that Kate and Thaddeas stood on the porch.

The rest of the evening developed around Mattie's dinner invitation of fried fish and hush puppies.

Ben was not about to lose any ground to

Thaddeas, so he graciously accepted Mattie's invitation. Oblivious to Ben's intentions, Kate sniffed the delicious fish and thought, *How perfect the day has turned out after all.*

CHAPTER 21

"All I'm saying is you don't need to upset the apple cart, Dan. We want to make a good impression on the Reverend," Rose Whitfield warned her husband and pointed her finger sternly.

"Don't go getting your nose out of joint, Rose. I won't muddy the waters as long as the subject don't come up!" Dan Whitfield stuck to his ground.

"Well, I never! You know the subject of savages isn't fit for the supper table anyway. Perhaps you could bring up the Reverend's wedding. It might put a notion in Ben's head. No harm laying the proper groundwork now, is there?" Rose stooped over to eye the side of the table, and then moved her plump body forward, giving the table covering a tug to set it straight.

"More like setting a trap," Dan retorted, shaking his head.

"Now, Dan, you know that none of you

fellas would offer for a lady unless properly baited. That's the charm of it." She walked over to give him a playful squeeze.

"They're here!" cried Melanie, peering out the sitting room window.

"All right, Daughter. Act like a lady now. Pa, answer the door."

At supper, Rose seated Melanie beside Ben. He glanced across the table and did not miss the smirk on Luke's face.

"It's mighty good of you to be weddin' the widow Potter," Rose addressed the Reverend and waited to see what he had to say for himself.

"Oh, it's not charity, I assure you! I'm quite fond of Mary and her boys. It will do us bachelors good to have a woman in the house."

"Really! Well, try some of this berry pie, Reverend. My Melanie baked it. I don't like to brag, but she's a wonderful cook. I reckon she'll do a man proud some day," she added, looking directly at Ben and winking.

"Mama, really!" Melanie exclaimed in mock humility. Then she teased, "However, I predict another wedding shortly."

"Whose?" Luke was the first to fall for the bait.

"Kate and Thaddeas!" she announced saucily.

Luke choked on his water, and Ben squirmed in his seat under the steady gaze of Rose Whitfield.

The room became still, and Rose picked up on the comment. "They do make sech a lovely couple . . . as long as Thaddeas knows what he's getting into. From what I hear, Kate breaks hearts like Mattie makes dresses, a new one for every occasion. She likes to toy with men's affections. Probably gets it honest enough. Look how long the sheriff's courted Mattie, and she still refuses to tie the knot. More pie, anyone?"

Ben thought about Sunday, how Thaddeas had ruined his visit. *What a fool I am!* Then the mention of Kate's name snapped him back to the present.

"Kate seems like a real nice girl to me, Rose," the Reverend said sternly. "I think whatever you heard is just the product of someone's active imagination."

"Well, some things just do set tongues a-wagging, Reverend," she retorted.

Later on the ride home, the Reverend said, "I hate to see Mattie and Kate's names darkened, but the Whitfields are teetering on the edge of the totter. I must be careful not to offend them and turn them away from the church when they need Jesus."

Luke spoke angrily, "It appears they come to Sunday meeting with the sole purpose of marrying Melanie to Ben."

CHAPTER 22

At the Potters', Mary put a pot of coffee on the fire and scrutinized the cabin, planning in her head. She ached to do some heavy work and burn off the restlessness that stemmed from waiting. Movement through the window caught her eye. She rushed out the door and greeted Mattie with a hug. "Come on in and have yourselves some coffee," she invited.

"I thought we came to work," Mattie said, laughing.

"That, too. There's plenty of that! I didn't know how much belongin's we had until I started to rummage through things. We can start in the kitchen. I won't be takin' all my cookin' kettles and such; some we'll just have ta leave."

At the Wheelers', things commenced along the same lines. Ben and Luke rearranged their room to fit both beds and all their belongings into a small space. "Maybe if we

hang a few pegs here for your clothes . . . ,"
Luke suggested. "Aw, shucks, why don't you
get married; then we wouldn't have to bunk
together," he teased.

"Don't hold your breath a-waiting."

Luke knew Ben was upset since their dinner at the Whitfields. "What you need is
more determination." Ben's back was
turned, and when he did not respond, Luke
continued. "If you care about Kate, you
have to go after her."

"I don't believe I asked for your advice,
little brother," Ben snapped.

"Aw, simmer down now. I don't want to
scrap."

"How are you boys doing in there?" called
the Reverend.

"Fine, Pa," Ben said. "Come on in, if you
can get in."

"No, I'm headed to Mary's to load up her
things. Wanted you to know I was leaving."

The afternoon dragged for Ben, who knew
Kate was returning with the wagons. Finally,
a cloud of dust appeared in the distance.

"Here they come," Luke said with a tinge
of dread. "Things will never be the same as
they were."

Everyone pitched in, and the Potters'
belongings were soon in place. James and
Frank were elated that they would soon be

kin to Ben and Luke, whom they idolized.

Kate looked wistfully about the cabin at Mary's belongings lovingly placed here and there. She thought it looked cozy.

Mary planned to stay with Mattie until the wedding. The next day, preparations would take place for the wedding itself, which was to be held at Tucker House.

The Reverend looked at Ben and Luke. "One of you boys want to take the ladies home?"

Ben's face turned pink, but he did not offer. Luke could not believe how stubborn his brother was acting. "I'll go, Father," Luke said.

On the ride home Kate had ample time to sulk. Ben had ignored her all day, and she knew he did it intentionally. Why was he angry? She racked her brain, trying to recall his last visit.

The wagon squeaked to a stop, and Luke helped Mattie and Mary to the ground. Annabelle and Claire jumped off the back when he came around to help Kate. Tired, they made their way toward the house after offering Luke thanks. Luke hesitated a moment and then called out, "Kate!"

She wanted to be left alone, but she turned toward him. "Yes?" She noticed the worried look that set creases in his freckled face and felt ashamed. "Something on your mind, Luke?"

"I may be sticking my nose where it does not belong. . . ."

Kate smiled. "What are you trying to say?"

"Don't be too hard on Ben." Her brows arched in surprise. "He was rude to you today, but he's got a case of green fever."

"I don't understand."

Her look of innocence encouraged him to stick out his neck even further. "Do you care for Thaddeas?" Kate could not believe this conversation was taking place. "As a suitor?" Luke probed.

"No, of course not," Kate replied, shaking her head.

"Ben has the crazy idea that you do. He's sick with jealousy. There, now I've said it, and he would skin me alive if he knew. Good day, Kate."

Kate watched him ride away in disbelief. Ben was jealous. He cared! Lifting her skirts, she ran toward the creek. She felt alive. At the top of the ridge with the water swirling below her, she shouted, "Ben cares! He cares!"

Slowly she dropped to the ground and looked toward heaven. She remembered Ben's sullenness and hurt. "Oh, Father," she prayed, "what shall I do?"

CHAPTER 23

September 20, the Reverend's wedding day, dawned warm and sweet. The Reverend looked elegant enough in his new gray suit. His snow-white hair was newly cut and topped with a dapper gray hat to match. James and Frank were dressed in new linen shirts, feeling stiff and starched in their buttoned-up collars. Ben and Luke looked handsome in their Sunday best.

Mary wore a pale blue dress that brought out the sky in her eyes. Her fingers lingered as she touched the white lacework that danced circles on her dainty round collar. The material was the prettiest she had ever laid eyes on, soft as a kitten and delightful to the touch. It was a gift from her betrothed. He ordered it from Dayton via Cooper's and hired Mattie to design and sew it, a luxury which Mary would never have afforded herself.

Outside, colorful leaves floated to the

earth to carpet the wedding floor. Sheriff Larson and Thaddeas were in charge as folks gathered.

The Reverend shook hands and received blessings as he walked to the big hickory tree where they were to be married. Ben and Luke stood toward the front of the crowd and waited while Mattie, Kate, and the girls took their honored place.

Ben stole a glance and thought Kate looked like an angel in a very pale green dress with a big bow in the back and a full flowing skirt. Her long black hair hung in curls with flowers for adornment.

The crowd turned as Mary approached, escorted by her young sons. A hush fell over the crowd. Mary's face radiated love's bloom, a flower lovely and sweet. Everyone knew the sorrows she had experienced and rejoiced with her in this newfound love and family being created. Everything went just as planned as the circuit preacher gave a short sermon on marriage.

Kate's eyes searched Ben's a few times, but he stared straight ahead. The couple repeated their vows and sealed them with a kiss. Afterward there was a fabulous feast. The fiddlers got out their instruments, and the newlyweds celebrated to the sound of lively music as couples paired off to dance the quadrille.

"Afternoon, Ben." Melanie looked radiant in a yellow gown that complemented her golden hair. "Such a lovely wedding," she sighed. The music boomed too loud for talking, which suited Ben fine.

Tanner approached Kate with a woman on his arm. "You've met Elizabeth?"

"Of course. How lovely you look," Kate replied with a smile.

Tanner took courage and spoke out. "This wedding seems like a good place to announce that we plan to tie the knot soon, too. We just need to talk with the Reverend. Elizabeth gave me her answer last night."

Kate squeezed Tanner's hand. "I'm so happy for you, Tanner." She turned to give Elizabeth a hug to show that all was forgiven.

"Well, how about that!" Melanie exclaimed, watching on. "I guess Thaddeas won't have to worry about Tanner anymore."

"Let's not talk about them," Ben grunted.

"They make such a lovely couple. Look! They're dancing."

"Would you care for something to drink, Melanie?" Ben asked while leading her away from the crowd. He burned with jealousy.

■ ■ ■ ■

"Kate?" Thaddeas said. "I have a confession to make."

"You do? What is it, Thaddeas?"

"You're very beautiful; in fact, the first time I saw you, I was deeply shook." Kate stiffened. "Buck keeps telling me that I should pursue you."

"Thaddeas!" She must stop this talk at once.

"But my heart is elsewhere."

"What? It is?"

"As much as I come calling, I thought I'd better clear the air. I wouldn't want you to get the wrong idea."

"I see."

"I'm sorry, Kate, but my heart is set on Annabelle."

"What! Annabelle! Why, she's just a child."

"I know, but I have plenty of time to wait."

Ben tried to keep his eye on Kate and Thaddeas, and noticed they were in deep conversation when he was interrupted by Luke.

"Determination, Brother . . . you need more determination."

Melanie's eyes followed their gaze and rested on Kate and Thaddeas. "I wonder what makes a girl behave like that? Anyone can see you're smitten with her, yet she flaunts Thaddeas under your nose. I would never treat you that way, Ben."

"Why, that's sweet of you to say, Melanie, but I think you're too hard on her," Ben said without taking his eyes off the couple.

"How can you defend her?"

Melanie turned in exasperation to glare at Luke, and he just shrugged his shoulders. As she marched off, he muttered under his breath, "That's it, Brother, determination!"

Meanwhile Thaddeas went on, "I have to get established, get started in business, save up some money. I've got plenty of time. She isn't thinking about romance yet, I know, but I'm willing to wait until she's older."

"I–I wish you well, Thaddeas," Kate said, not sure how to reply to this astonishing news.

"You're not upset, are you, Kate?"

"Of course not." *Twice in one day!* she thought. *I've been dumped twice today by men I don't even love.*

"Do you suppose she'd dance with me?"

Kate nodded.

"Mind if I cut in, Thaddeas?" Ben towered over them.

"Not at all." He gave Ben a big grin and nudged his way through the throng to look for Annabelle.

Kate's heart was a wicked beating drum. *I may not get another chance like this.* Her lips trembled. "Ben?"

When he looked into her soft brown eyes, his mind flashed back to the day he had taken her to his farm, and he remembered her excitement about starting a church. He recalled her sweet spirit on that first Sunday. How could he doubt her? She might love Thaddeas, but she was not a heartbreaker.

"Kate, I'm sorry. I've treated you badly."

"No need to apologize. I understand."

"You do?"

She nodded.

"Could I call on you this week?"

On the way home, Luke reflected. "A lot of changes have come our way since we left Virginia."

"Yeah, when we were back on that flatboat crossing the Ohio River, I never dreamed Pa would get married again," Ben replied.

"I'm feeling a bit restless. I think maybe it's time for me to go back to school . . . get ready to start my ministry and all."

"I had a feeling you were going to leave us pretty soon. I'm gonna miss you something terrible!"

CHAPTER 24

Mattie, Kate, and Annabelle toiled in the garden. Now that the wedding was over, it was time to give it the attention it sorely needed. They turned most everything under except the big round pumpkins still growing on winding vines. The days were cool and brisk, but the hard work still made them thirsty and hot. Mattie sent Annabelle after water. Kate stood and put her fist in the small of her back to work out the kinks as she stretched with one arm and then the other. "On a day like today, it's good to be alive," she said.

"Yes, it is," Mattie replied absentmindedly. "Kate, let's invite company for Annabelle's birthday; she'll soon be fourteen."

"What a good idea! Who shall we invite?"

Just then the door slammed shut; Annabelle approached with a pitcher of cool water. "Think on it; we'll talk later," Mattie said quickly.

Annabelle giggled as she looked at Kate and Mattie. "Do you realize how dirty you two are?"

"I reckon you were just as dirty till ya just now cleaned up, weren't ya?" Mattie teased back.

"Nope, I didn't have a big smudge on my face like that." She scooped a handful of soil and wiped her dirty hands across Kate's face.

"Why, you!" Kate said, grabbing for Annabelle and missing. Annabelle shot off like a cannonball, running to the edge of the garden while Kate picked up a dirt clod and hurled it, hitting her right in the back.

"Ouch! Hey, that's not fair!" Annabelle knelt down to get her own ammunition while another clod buzzed high overhead. She stood up, but instead of pitching it at Kate, she threw it at an unsuspecting target, Mattie.

Smack! "What? Oh, you're in trouble now, Girl," Mattie cried.

Several minutes later they drank the water Annabelle had brought. "Whew! I'm gettin' too old for this," Mattie complained. "I think we've done enough for today. By the time we clean up and get dinner on, it'll be time for Claire ta come home."

"May I go to meet her?" Annabelle begged.

"Yes, that would be fine."

With Annabelle gone, Kate and Mattie talked about Annabelle's birthday.

"Let's surprise her!"

"Ya think we could?" Mattie asked. "Pull it off, I mean?"

"It would take some planning, but it would be fun."

"I reckon it could be done; let's do it!" Mattie agreed.

"Who should we invite?"

"The young folks about her age? Maybe we could get Ben and Thaddeas to take a couple of wagons, pick 'em all up, and deliver them home again so their folks don't have ta tote 'em all," Mattie suggested.

"This is going to be such fun; I can hardly wait!" Kate exclaimed.

"Sure . . . they could throw some hay in the wagon and let the kids have fun. Annabelle could get in on the hayride when they take the children home."

When Ben arrived for supper that night, he suggested that they take a walk, and that suited Kate. She grabbed her sweater off the peg in the kitchen and joined him.

"How are things going at your place?" she asked.

"Different, that's for sure!" Ben said. "It's hard to find any quiet. There's usually commotion during dinner with James and Frank horsing around. After dinner Mary and Pa visit. If I go to my room, Luke's in there. If I go to do chores, the boys follow me."

"I know what it's like to be around chatterboxes; it gets pretty lively around Tucker House. But I can always go to my room or sneak off to the creek, or out to the hickory tree. Do they follow you everywhere?" she asked.

"Well, not everywhere; sometimes they follow Luke," he said with a chuckle. Then, "Don't get me wrong; I shouldn't be complaining because they're good boys, and there's lots of love being shared around home. It's a good feeling. It's been a long time since Pa's been happy like this."

"That's good. I'm sure it'll work out in time."

"Luke's going to be leaving for school soon. I guess I'll have a room to myself then. I sure hate to see him go. We've always been close."

They stopped walking then and sat on a large log. As Kate gathered her skirts in her hand and spread them out about her in a perfect circle, she remembered her surprise. "Mattie and I are planning a birthday surprise for Annabelle." She shared the plan, and he volunteered to help.

"Will Thaddeas come?" he ventured.

"We plan to ask him, but we haven't seen him since the wedding. He usually comes over pretty often with the sheriff."

"So I've noticed. Answer a question for me? Does Thaddeas come calling on you? Courting . . . I mean?"

"No. We're only friends. As a matter of fact . . ."

"What?"

"Oh, Ben, I can't tell you. It's a secret."

"Tell me, Kate," Ben pleaded.

"Thaddeas has his heart set on Annabelle."

"Annabelle!" Ben exclaimed in surprise.

"Yes, now hush. Don't tell the world! He knows she's too young and aims to wait for her. Anyway, we're just friends. He needs friends, being from the East, and all."

"Annabelle!" Ben said again, shaking his head in disbelief. "He's looking at Annabelle when you live in the same house. I find that hard to believe."

"Well, believe it! Anyway, I don't care about him like that, even if he were to look my way."

"You don't know how glad I am to hear you say that. Ever since that first Sunday when he came to church with you, I've been crazy with jealousy."

"You have?" Ben nodded and looked at the ground. "Well, whenever Melanie comes around, I turn green," Kate confessed. "She made a special trip to Tucker House to tell me that you had dinner with them and how charming you were."

"Aw-shucks, she ain't nothing to me, Kate. Why does she bother you?"

"I recall you've danced with her more than once."

"You danced with Thaddeas!" With this outburst they broke into hearty laughter.

"I guess we've been a couple of fools," Ben admitted as a wave of contentment settled over him.

"Yes, we have."

"Kate? I wonder if dancing is such a good idea. Sure brings the worst out in people. Remember Tanner on Independence Day? Pa said some folks don't even participate . . . that they think dancing is wrong because it causes many evils."

"I never thought about it before, Ben."

"It sure seemed right when I was holding you," Ben admitted as his freckled face turned pink. "But I don't hold to the thought of you dancing with anyone else."

"I wonder how married folks feel about it?" Kate asked.

"I reckon some don't care, but I know I would!" Ben answered.

"I guess it's one of those things everyone has to decide for themselves."

"Yeah, I reckon so."

"I'm glad you came tonight, Ben."

"Me, too. May I call on you again?"

Kate nodded. "Now," she said, "let's talk about Annabelle's party!"

CHAPTER 25

October 10 blew in a very cold day. It fell on Friday, which was perfect for the surprises concocted for Annabelle's birthday.

She awoke to the aroma of birthday cake, which was a ploy to keep her off track. She chattered excitedly throughout breakfast, trying to discover what the day held.

Mattie said that she would have to wait until evening to open her gift. In her excitement, evening seemed days away. Mattie laughed at the pathetic expression on Annabelle's face. Then according to plan, Mattie suggested that she spend the day with Dorie Cooper in town. Annabelle was ecstatic. To spend a whole day with Dorie would be splendid indeed! Dorie always knew the latest gossip, the latest fads, and the most up-to-date styles. Sometimes they studied catalogs filled with new merchandise that Mr. Cooper used to purchase supplies. And, of course, they shared secrets and dreams.

Claire was in on the surprise, but put on a convincing act, portraying the disappointed child, going to school while Annabelle had such an entertaining day with Dorie.

With Annabelle finally out the door and Claire off to school, Kate and Mattie hustled to get everything in order for the festivities that evening. The day flew by, and they tried to act as normal as possible when Annabelle returned for supper that evening. They all listened as she told about her day with Dorie and thanked them over and over again for letting her go. They made a big hoopla out of the birthday cake and showered her with hugs and kisses.

Mattie disappeared and came back carrying a brown package. "Happy Birthday!" she said as she presented it to Annabelle. It was small but heavy for its size. She shook it carefully and after lengthy examination tore open the brown paper wrappings.

"Oh!" she exclaimed in delight. "How lovely." It was a small glass dish with flowers boldly painted on the lid, just the right size to store precious trinkets.

After the dishes were washed, Mattie started a fire in the fireplace, and they all gathered in the sitting room, listening to the wind's howl outside. Annabelle rambled on with recollections of the day. All of a sudden, they heard a terrible commotion.

"I wonder what that could be?" Mattie said, and they all moved to the window and jerked the curtains aside to peer out. Two lights bobbed like stars in the darkness. They were the flickering lanterns from two wagons, loaded with folks making a loud racket.

"What in the world?" Mattie exclaimed as the three girls crowded in close to see what was happening. Two already knew, and one was being totally taken in.

As the wagons drew nearer, the young folks yelled wildly, "Annabelle! Annabelle! We want Annabelle!"

Annabelle still did not comprehend, and Claire clapped with delight. One more look at Mattie and Kate and understanding dawned. "Oh! Oh!" Annabelle joined Claire in clapping, and then picked up her skirts and ran outside. The young folks piled out and grabbed and hugged her until she was totally overcome with sentiment.

Ben and Thaddeas worked together and made a fire in spite of the gusty wind. The young folks gathered around them. "Dorie, you scamp! You knew all the time, didn't you? Shame on you for tricking me!" Annabelle scolded.

"I thought sure I'd burst, keeping it inside

all day." Dorie giggled.

Mattie brought out corn to pop over the fire and cider for the young folks to drink. There were nine young people, all of Annabelle's favorites. The girls had brought small gifts and demanded that Annabelle open them immediately. The adults kept a special eye out for Bart and Andy, two older boys known for their ornery pranks. Thaddeas noticed that Bart and Andy were not living up to their reputation of roughhousing. Instead they kept their eyes on the girls, especially Annabelle and Dorie. *They must be growing up,* Thaddeas thought.

Thaddeas felt frustrated over the age difference between himself and Annabelle. Sometimes she was a young lady, and other times she was still a child. *At least this birthday makes her one year older,* he thought dismally.

A few hours later, Annabelle and her friends had settled down and gathered around the fire where they chatted quietly. "I hate to break it up, especially now that it's quieted down, but I reckon we should be getting these young people back to their folks," Ben whispered to Kate.

"Yes, I suppose you're right," Kate said dreamily. "It's been a good party."

"I was hoping that you would ride along."

"I'd love to go. Let me get a couple of blankets while you round up everybody. I'll tell Mattie the plan," Kate replied.

Soon they were jostling down the road, hardly able to talk with all of the horseplay and laughter coming from behind. Kate was content, happy that the surprise had worked and Annabelle was having such a fine time. The young folks sang some songs. Then they became quieter, snuggling down in the hay and giggling.

"Are you warm enough, Kate?" Ben asked.

"Yes, warm from the inside out," she replied, hoping that he would understand her intended meaning.

He did, as those in love are apt to cling hopelessly to every real or imagined gesture of endearment.

The wagons pulled to a stop to let Sammy off at the Hawkes' place. The boy jumped off the wagon, gave a wave, and headed for his house. Just then Annabelle noticed he had left his cap lying in the hay. She jumped up to yell after him. At the same time, Thaddeas started the team to pull ahead. The movement caught Annabelle by surprise, and she lost her balance and fell, head first, over the side of the wagon.

What followed was a blur. Someone

screamed and yelled, and Thaddeas stopped the team to find the trouble. When he understood, he jumped down frantically, giving the reins to Bart. He found Annabelle lying on the road. He was sure her arm was broken, hit by the wagon wheel. The worst was the puddle of blood under her limp head. She did not respond in any way, and Thaddeas was too distraught to think clearly.

By the time Ben and Kate got there, Thaddeas was holding her saying, "Annabelle, oh, Annabelle, what have I done?"

Ben quickly took charge. "She's breathing," he said. Kate felt her chest cave in, so awesome was the weight of the horror in it. Annabelle, so full of life one moment, now lay lifeless and pale. Kate knelt down beside Annabelle as Claire sobbed uncontrollably.

"I need a clean cloth to stop the bleeding," Ben said to Kate. "She has a cut. How about your petticoat?"

She pulled up her skirt and tried to rip a piece, but it would not tear. Ben reached over and with one swift motion managed to tear the delicate cotton petticoat. Then he tore it into two long strips. He folded one to make a pad and pressed it against her wound. "Hold this tight," he ordered, and Kate did as she was told. Then he took another strip and wrapped it around Annabelle's head to hold the pad in place.

"Thaddeas?"

Thaddeas nodded where he stood, wringing his hands.

"Get all the young folks into one wagon. Finish dropping them off, and try and get them calmed down. We'll put Kate, Claire, and Annabelle in the other wagon, and head for Doc Malone's. Stop in at Tucker House on the way back to get Mattie if I haven't already been there. See you back at Doc Malone's. Are you all right?"

"No, but I know what needs to be done. Thanks, Ben."

All Kate remembered of the ride to the doctor's was the awful blackness that draped the night's sky and the deafening howl of the wind. She held Claire so tightly that the two seemed as one in the midst of it all.

CHAPTER 26

The waiting seemed like an eternity, sitting in Doc Malone's small outer room while the doctor and his wife worked fervently over Annabelle, who lay motionless on the big bed in the other room. The small circle of friends comforted each other as best they could while tragedy stalked mercilessly nearby.

Death's presence could be felt, an unseen yet powerful enemy, draping them in a shroud of helplessness. Kate bowed her head in response, seeking her comforter, Jesus, but she quickly jerked it up again as she heard a creaking sound. The door to the adjoining room was opening! She drew a long breath and held it, waiting. . . .

The doctor limped into the room. He ran his hands through his hair, and Kate saw beads of perspiration on his brow.

"It's not good," he said. Huge tears rolled down Mattie's pale cheeks uncontrollably, and Sheriff Larson reached over and lightly gripped her shoulder. "She had a broken arm; we set it. That'll be fine in time . . . some scrapes and bruises, we cleaned them. There was a nasty cut on the back of her head where she must have hit a rock. Whoever stopped the bleeding probably saved her life."

Thaddeas leaned forward, placed his elbows on his knees, and cupped his head in his hands. Then he shook his head as if in disbelief that this could all really be happening.

The doctor continued, "We put twenty-five stitches in mending it, and we had to shave some of her head. But the part that's bad is the bump on her temple. It's responsible for her unconscious state. The good part is that she's stirring, although delirious. There's just no saying if she'll come out of it or not. If she makes it through the night, her chances are better. We'll just have to wait it out and pray. I know the Lord heals folks. I've seen plenty of miracles in my lifetime."

"I believe He will," Kate said. "I just know He will."

"I suggest that Mattie stay and the rest of you go home."

"Maybe I should get Pa," Ben offered.

"No need," Mattie said coldly.

Ben looked confused at the tone of her voice. "We'll be praying just the same, and I'm sure he'll want to come in the morning," he assured her. She did not reply but sat stiffly, staring at the bedroom door.

The sheriff said, "Best do as Doc says. I'll stay here the night and keep an eye on Mattie." Kate nodded in agreement.

"Come on, Thaddeas. We'll drop you off," Ben offered.

First, they dropped Thaddeas off at the sheriff's place. Ben walked him to the door. "Are you all right, Friend?" Ben asked.

Thaddeas's reserve crumbled. "It's all my fault . . . it's my fault that she fell out of the wagon, and then . . . and then, I ran over her." Ben placed his arms around Thaddeas, supporting him until the moment of weakness passed.

"Thaddeas, it's not your fault at all. Annabelle stood up, and it was an accident. That's all. It could have happened to any one of those youngsters on my wagon."

"But Annabelle . . . why Annabelle?" Thaddeas moaned.

"Why don't you come on home with me tonight, Thaddeas. I hate to see you like this."

"No, no. I'll be all right. It's just that there

is nothing I can do."

"You can pray, Thaddeas."

He nodded. "I'll do that. Thanks, Ben."

As Ben walked back to the wagon, he noticed Thaddeas was not lighting any lamps, just leaving the house dark. *That would be me, if something happened to Kate.*

He climbed back onto the wagon seat. The night was cold. Claire shivered, tightly squeezed between Kate and Ben on the seat. "It'll be all right, Claire," he patted her cold little hands. They drove on, and Kate cried silently, staring into black nothingness.

Ben went into Tucker House with Kate and Claire, lit the candle just inside the door, and then one of the lamps. "I'll stay if you want," he offered.

Kate managed a weak smile and shook her head. "Your pa will be worried. You'd better go on home."

"Only if you're sure you'll be all right."

"I'm sure," she said. Then, as if remembering something, she suddenly called out, "Ben?" He was immediately at her side. "Thank you so much. What would we have done without you?"

She looked so vulnerable holding Claire's frail hand, her lips quivering. Ben reached out and pulled them both to his breast, holding them in a tight embrace. Then he released them and smiled tenderly.

"I'll be by in the morning to take you back to the doc's."

Kate nodded, and he turned, pulled his hat on tightly, and was out the door.

"Are you hungry or thirsty, Claire?" she asked. Claire shook her head. "Let's go up to bed then." Kate lit the candle again and turned out the lamp. "Would you like to sleep with me tonight, Claire?" The young girl nodded that she would.

As Kate lay in bed, enveloped in the bleakness of night, she found herself listening to Claire's soft breathing in comparison to the heavy wind blowing outside. She tried to put some perspective into her thinking. *How can the world be so perfect one minute and so dark the next? Life can be good or cruel,* she thought. She remembered again being a little girl in the root cellar, the Indian raid, and holding Annabelle. . . . *Oh, Annabelle.*

Some things are out of man's control; like the way love bubbles up from within for a special person, coloring the world rosy, or the way we are all so fragile and can face death at any moment. Yet one thing remains constant, God's love.

"Oh, Jesus," she prayed. "I don't know if

Annabelle is ready to meet you. It's not her fault, Lord . . . with our folks dying when she was so young and Mattie rebelling against you. Please, Jesus, give her another chance and heal her body." Kate prayed whenever she woke as she drifted in and out of a restless slumber.

Mattie could not sleep. She just stared at the bedroom door. Once Mrs. Malone came out to check her, and Mattie asked if she could go sit by Annabelle's side.

"All right, for a little while, but then you must try to get some rest, Mattie. If she comes around tomorrow, she'll need you."

The next morning, bright and early, Ben and his pa headed for Beaver Creek.

"Looks like another windy day, but the sun sure warms a body up," the Reverend said. "It reminds me of God's steadfast love when times are hard." Ben nodded, and then they rode on silently.

Meanwhile, Kate started a fire and tempted Claire with some warm oatmeal. Having Claire to take care of helped keep up her courage. They were anxious for the Wheelers to come and take them to the doctor's, but Kate was still surprised and grateful when they arrived so early. She moved methodically to the door to let them in.

The Reverend reached for her right away, and she fell into his arms. "Well, are you girls ready to go to the doctor's?" he asked. Kate nodded, and they grabbed their wraps off the peg behind the door and headed out. As they drove into Beaver Creek, all sorts of thoughts raced through their minds — thoughts of hope and trusting chased by thoughts of despair and fear.

Soon they pulled up outside of the doctor's house. The Wheelers helped the girls down and led them to the door. Ben paused a moment while everyone searched inside for courage, and then they entered.

The sheriff sat on the settee drinking coffee. He shook his head as if to say nothing had changed. Mrs. Malone popped her head out of the kitchen and rushed to greet them. She shook their hands warmly and took their wraps. "Here, sit down," she said, and motioned toward some chairs.

"May I go in and see them?" the Reverend asked.

"Yes, that would be fine," answered the doctor who had just limped into the room. "There's been no change with Annabelle except her head is more swollen, and Mattie's taking it so hard. She just sits and stares. She won't rest, and she doesn't talk. It's natural and all. . . . Everyone takes grief differently, but I hope you can help, Reverend."

"I'll see what I can do."

"Mattie, I'm sorry," the Reverend said as he entered the dark room. He walked to where she was sitting and took one of her limp hands into his own. She jerked, and her body went rigid. Mattie looked at the Reverend with cold, hard eyes. "I want to help you if I can," he went on.

She pulled her hand away and jumped to her feet. "Then you just tell God ta leave me alone! He's took and took from me . . . until there's nothing left ta give. How can He be so cruel?" she screamed.

"Mattie, I know it seems like that, but He hasn't taken Annabelle. We can't be blaming Him. We need to be seeking Him, asking Him to help us."

"Well . . . He won't help me; I know that! I ain't countin' on His help!"

"May I just kneel here and pray silently for Annabelle?"

"Do what ya want. I'll go get some coffee." She turned abruptly and left the room, walking with shoulders slumped into the sitting room. Kate went to her immediately, noticing the deep dark circles under her swollen eyes.

In the other room, the Reverend kneeled

beside Annabelle's bed, praying for her healing, and praying for wisdom and insight. Then he nodded and prayed for Mattie, praying that her heart would be softened and she might come to terms with her Maker.

CHAPTER 27

When the Reverend got up from his knees that morning, he opened his eyes and looked around the room, perhaps expecting to hear directly from God. No dramatic revelation or healing miracle took place within the Malones' bedroom. He only saw the sun's rays, shining in through the windows and splattering warmth across him and the wooden slats on the floor.

He stood and looked once more at the beautiful young girl lying on the big bed and felt his own weakness and need to depend on God. He knew he should pray for Mattie as well as Annabelle. He believed God was listening.

Anyone as old as the Reverend was not sheltered from the frailties of human life. He had seen people suffer and die and had been called upon to bear these burdens with them. His own dear first wife had faded away like the light at the end of day. Yet over the years, his faith in God's goodness and healing power had grown. After all, God also healed people. Many verses in the Bible told about God wanting the best for His people. The Reverend believed that God could use this accident to accomplish good for His children if they would only turn to Him in their time of need.

Most of God's promises had conditions connected to them, and Romans 8:28 was not any different: "And we know that all things work together for good to them that love God, to them who are the called according to his purpose." He knew that if Mattie did not love God, He would not be able to perform His will in this, so the Reverend resolved to pray for Mattie constantly in the days ahead.

When he came out of the bedroom, Mattie agreed to let the sheriff take her home where she could rest while Kate stayed with Annabelle.

Claire asked, "Please, Mattie, before we leave, may I see Annabelle?"

"I'll go in with her," Kate added.

"All right," Mattie said, "I'll wait outside." She turned and walked wearily out the door, followed by her devoted sheriff.

When Kate and Claire entered Annabelle's room, they walked timidly up to the bedside. Kate placed her hand on Annabelle's broken arm.

"Oh, poor Annabelle," Claire said.

"She's sleeping."

"Kate?"

"Yes."

"Do you think God really hears us when we pray?"

"Yes, I really think so, Claire."

"Will he wake Annabelle up if we ask Him?"

"I hope so, Claire. That's what I've been asking Him to do. I trust God to do the best thing for Annabelle. I know He loves her as much as we do."

"How do you know that?"

"It says so in the Bible, Claire," Kate said, bringing Claire's small delicate hand up now, and pressing it to her breast.

"I'd do anything for God if He'd let Annabelle wake up," said Claire.

"Claire, you need to be strong today . . . for Mattie's sake. Do you know what I mean?"

"Yes, Kate."

"Are you ready to go now?"

"Yes, bye, Annabelle. Please wake up . . . we need you, Annabelle."

Kate led Claire out of the room and watched her leave. Then she turned back to the bedside to start her vigil.

Meanwhile, Doc Malone told the Wheelers, "There is no way of knowing for sure, but Annabelle probably will be unconscious until the swelling goes down on her head. She started with a fever early this morning, and I hope that when it breaks, she'll awaken."

The next few days were days of waiting and trying to keep the fever down. Annabelle did not respond to the world around her, other than sporadic movements and words that indicated she was having some dreams in her own world, far away.

Kate and Mattie took turns at her bedside with Mrs. Malone and the doctor always doing their best. Many friends dropped in at Tucker House to comfort those who they would find at home, or at the doctor's house to see if there was anything they could do to help. The Reverend called daily at the Malones', and if he did not find Mattie there, he also would stop in at Tucker House.

Mattie was never so rude to him again as she had been that first morning, but her former smile was replaced by a face set in stone. Thus she continued to withdraw from her family and friends more each day, refusing their comfort and solace.

Ben did his best to encourage and support Kate. He knew it was a hard time for her. She was not aware of what she said or did during those days, but Ben was aware. He watched her in admiration. His heart grew fonder toward her as he valued her inner character, her faith, courage, and compassion. A precious jewel, he desired with all his heart to make this remarkable woman his own.

One afternoon, exactly four days after the accident, kneeling on the cold, hard floor in her room, Claire petitioned God. "I know You are Kate's God. But if You'll help my sister, I'll have You for my God, too. Kate said that You love Annabelle. If You let her wake up and make her well again, I'll promise to serve You. I'll be whatever You want, a preacher . . . a nurse . . . or a missionary. I promise. Amen."

That little prayer hinged on the edge of hope and a turn of events. In the meantime, Mattie returned to Doc Malone's to sit once more with Annabelle. As she entered the room, she was overcome by a sense of helplessness. She felt like a speck of dust in the mighty universe and like her circumstances were of no concern to God . . . if there was a God. She slumped in a chair under the window and waited for Annabelle to regain consciousness.

"Mattie, the swelling is down, and the fever is broken," the Reverend told her.

"She ain't never comin' back, though, is she?"

"Why, I was just thinking she would, any hour now. The doctor said this is the most crucial time. He said that . . ."

Mattie interrupted. "It's all so useless."

"What? What's useless, Mattie?"

"What other people think, what other people say, all the prayin'; none of it changes anythin', does it now?"

"It does for me, Mattie. Maybe you just aren't receiving."

"What do ya mean?"

"I don't mean to be showing disrespect, Mattie, but you're building a wall and not letting anyone through it. You can't be encouraged, supported, or even loved if you don't allow it. You're shutting out your family and friends who love you so much. We want to help, Mattie."

"Love? Whenever I love . . . it hurts. I don't have enough courage to open up ta folks anymore."

"Sometimes love is pain, Mattie. God hurts when His people don't return His love. Jesus died on the cross because He loved us. Isn't that pain?"

With these words Mattie sobbed uncontrollably. "He doesn't love me. How could He?"

"Oh, Mattie, He does love you. I know He does."

"What? What's this?" a raspy weak voice whispered from behind them, so faintly that for a moment they were not really sure it was real.

Then they rushed to the bedside, Mattie trembling as she quickly dropped to her knees at Annabelle's side.

"Annabelle! Annabelle dear, we're here. Everything's all right, Dear. We're right here."

"W–where am I? W–what happened?"

"You had an accident, Dear. But you'll be fine, jest fine."

The doctor was immediately summoned, and he sent them all from the room for a time as he examined Annabelle.

As relief flowed through Mattie, it washed away the stony façade of detachment that had been her way of coping.

"Reverend," she said, "may I speak to ya?"

When Mattie came out of that room, she was transformed. Bitterness and fear fled, and God's Spirit did a wondrous work within her heart. She was filled with new courage and bubbled over with a newfound love and joy.

Hard times continued because even though Annabelle awoke from her state of unconsciousness, she was not herself. The family could see that but did not really know the extent of the problem yet. She acted incoherent, as though she did not know who they were or what they were talking about. The doctor said this was sometimes a normal reaction and she should improve as time went on. Vigils would still be kept at Doc Malone's, because she would not be able to be moved yet for a couple of days.

Much later Kate and Ben rode to Tucker House, quietly recalling all that had transpired that evening. Kate was deep in thought when she realized Ben was chuckling beside her.

"What's so funny?" she asked.

"Oh, I was just thinking of the expression on the sheriff's face tonight at the change in Mattie."

Kate smiled. "Yes, he was rather smitten, wasn't he?"

"Think they'll ever get together?"

"I don't know. They really think so much of each other; maybe there's a better chance now."

"He follows her around like a little puppy."

"And you don't think that's good?" Kate asked.

"It's just amusing to watch, that's all."

"Really?"

Ben reached over and took her hand, but did not share the things in his heart. There had been enough excitement for one evening, and he knew she was not really quite herself yet. He would wait until the time was right. Contentedly, they continued until they reached Tucker House.

After Ben was alone, though, his emotions got the better of him, and he exploded in a burst of song. The amazing thing was he did not even feel foolish as he rode home, singing at the top of his loud baritone voice in the dark of the night, while the stars twinkled God's approval.

CHAPTER 28

Thaddeas trotted his horse toward Tucker House to call on Annabelle and check her recovery since she had been moved home. *Perhaps familiar surroundings are just the thing she needs,* he thought, *to help her get her senses back. I hope so.* And he nudged his horse on. He had brought along some flowers for Annabelle and soon found himself on the Tucker House doorstep, posies in hand.

"Come in, Thaddeas," Kate said cheerfully. "How nice of you to stop by."

"The flowers are for Annabelle. . . . I should have thought to bring you some, too, Miss Kate," he stuttered.

"Nonsense! Annabelle's the one recuperating, not me. Come along, and I'll take you to her."

Annabelle heard the stair steps creak in protest and cheered that someone was coming up to see her. *Doesn't sound like those who have been attending to me,* she reasoned. *I wonder who it could be? Oh, why am I so confused?* It was frustrating when things were on the very edge of remembering, almost there, and then gone again. It was that way with names, faces, events. Just when she felt it was familiar and she thought she was remembering, she would go totally blank. She could not seem to focus. Everyone was kind enough, but she felt distraught and too weak and tired to do anything about it.

"Hello, Annabelle!" Thaddeas said with forced enthusiasm.

Annabelle looked at the young man standing before her. *What a nice-looking fellow,* she thought. *I wonder who he is?* Then, "Oh dear," she said aloud.

"Well, I am a dear. That's true enough, but I didn't know you were aware of it." He grinned.

"I'm sorry. Just trying to remember." Her eyes fastened fixedly on his handsome face.

He blushed under her steady gaze as Kate said, "Annabelle, this is Thaddeas, Thaddeas Larson. He is the sheriff's nephew." Then to Thaddeas she said, "I'll leave you to visit alone," turned, and was heard stepping lightly down the stairs.

"Well, Annabelle, please don't trouble yourself trying to remember me. I'm not an old friend, but indeed a good one."

She smiled at this and relaxed a bit to watch with fascination as he continued.

"I've only been in Beaver Creek a couple months, and as Kate said, I'm staying with the sheriff. But perhaps you'll remember I'm your fishing partner. One Sunday afternoon we went fishing at the creek." He paused to watch her reaction.

She shook her head sadly. "No," she said, "I'm sorry, but I don't seem to remember it at all. Do you pick flowers at the creek as well?"

Thaddeas laughed. "Well, your memory may be a little rusty, but your wit is certainly in fine tune. These are for you. Perhaps they will put me in your favor, and the next time I come to visit you, you will count me as a friend . . . a new friend . . . and one that you can count on, Annabelle."

As Thaddeas went to put them in a vase by the side of her bed, she asked, "Will you visit me again?"

"Of course! What are friends for?"

As she mulled this over, another scene developed in the room below. Kate went to the door again, and much to her astonishment, there stood Tanner.

"Hello, Tanner," Kate said, "please, come in."

"Thanks, Kate. Could we just talk outside?"

Kate followed Tanner, and they sat down on the porch step. She waited patiently until Tanner was ready to talk.

"What do you think of Elizabeth?"

"Why, she's very pretty, and she seems nice enough," Kate answered with embarrassment.

"Yeah, that's her. Took your advice, you know. I've got a lot to make up. Hope I can make her happy; I know she'll be good for me."

"I'm sure you'll both be very happy," Kate said, trying to reassure him.

"Aw . . . who am I trying to fool? I came here to tell you. I don't know what love is, but I think I love her," he blurted out.

Kate laughed. "I think you're finding out, Tanner."

"You're not mad, are you?" he asked, regaining his poise and shooting her one of his famous smiles.

"Tanner, I'm just so happy for you. I really am!" she said earnestly. "I'm most happy that you found the Lord!"

"Yeah, me, too. Luke's teaching me. He

comes over, and we study the Bible."

"Really? That's great!" Kate exclaimed.

"You know, the Reverend even had a dream about me?"

"Tell me about it."

"Well the Reverend said he was walking through a cornfield when the wind swept him up and set him down on the edge of a green pasture with sheep in it. A voice said, 'Feed My flock.' Then a lamb romped through and destroyed the corn.

"That was me, Kate . . . when I rode through their farm and shot things up. Well, it made him mad in his dream, and he yelled, 'Get out of my corn.' Then the voice said again, 'Feed My flock.' So he let the lamb go. When he did, other lambs followed, and the cornfield sprung up, unharmed.

"The Reverend said when he started the church, he obeyed the voice. I was the sheep. He said other lambs will follow. The Wheelers think that means my friend Jake will get saved. Luke's been praying for him."

Kate covered her mouth with her hand in amazement as she recognized the dream, and shook her head as tears rolled down her cheeks. "Oh, that's beautiful, Tanner!"

"Aw, now don't go crying again," he said affectionately.

"I'm sorry, Tanner. You've just made me so happy."

Just then the door flew open, and Thaddeas walked out. "Hello, Tanner," he said.

Tanner jumped up. "Hello, Thaddeas. Join us?"

"No, I was just on my way out, but thanks and good day to you." Sadness colored his voice, and he hurried off.

"He's been to visit Annabelle," Kate said softly.

"Taking it kinda hard, I see. I'm sorry, Kate. Well, I'd better be off, too. It was good to see you."

As Tanner walked away, Kate called after him, "Tanner!"

He turned and waited.

"I just wanted to tell you; you're a man I can respect." Tanner rode away feeling ten feet tall.

Upstairs alone in her room, Annabelle stared out the window, quietly crying as big teardrops fell, wetting her pillow.

CHAPTER 29

Bare and twisting, the branches reached toward the frosty window that held Claire and Annabelle's gaze as they sat on their bed whispering. "I wish I could go to school with you; perhaps then I could remember again."

"You were always glad to be out of the schoolroom," replied Claire.

"Well, I don't know why," Annabelle said glumly.

"Come on. We'd better hurry and get downstairs for breakfast; it's getting late," said Claire.

As they descended the steps, Claire said, "I'll be so glad when you can braid my hair again. Kate pulls too tight, and my poor head gets so sore. Of course, I don't want to bother Kate with complaining when everyone is so worried about you. I'm glad you're getting better."

"But I'm not, Claire! Everyone just seems

to pretend that I am, but I'm not!"

"You'll get your memory back soon enough. Don't worry, Annabelle."

The aroma of hot mush, cooking in a black kettle over the fire, tempted them. It tasted good with fresh bread, butter, and honey.

"Ben said that Luke will be visiting the schoolhouse today. He's going to share with the children about going into ministry and what he expects the university life will be like," Kate said.

Claire's interest piqued. "Ministry?"

"Yes, he's studying to be a preacher like his pa. I thought you knew that, Claire."

"Maybe I did and just forgot. I wasn't interested in that stuff until . . ." She stopped for a moment, catching herself, and then continued, "until now that I'm older."

Mattie nodded, exchanging amused glances with Kate. "Well, I'd better be off then." Claire bolted from the table and grabbed her coat off the peg.

"Whatever brought that about?" Mattie wondered as did the others.

Claire's feet scarcely hit the crunchy, frost-covered ground as she hurried off to school. Little halos, puffs of breath, preceded her as she walked along at a brisk pace, but she did not notice. She thought about Luke's visit. The promise she made to God excited her, and she had many questions. Perhaps today she would find some answers. As she reached the little schoolhouse, which looked warm and inviting, Claire opened the door, and a cheery fire popped and spit its greeting.

"My, you're early this morning, Claire," said Miss Forrester. "Would you like to help?"

"Sure!"

"Very well, then. You may take the slates from the shelf and place one on each of the desks."

"Will we be doing our regular work today, Miss Forrester?"

"Yes, however, I do happen to have a surprise planned for today," she added with a twinkle in her eye.

The classroom filled with wriggling bodies. The children removed their coats and hats and huddled around the welcoming fire. They rubbed and patted their hands to get the color back into them. Eventually they went to their seats, and class began.

The day seemed to drag for Claire. First, they did their sums, then reciting, followed by recess. After recess, Miss Forrester explained the cycle of seasons, pointing out the barren signs of winter. Claire shuddered as they talked about ice formations. Finally, it was lunchtime. Sammy Hawkes chased her above all the others in their game of tag.

Reluctantly, the children returned to the classroom, and Miss Forrester read a story about the bitter cold winter the first settlers experienced when they arrived on the Mayflower. As Claire watched her squint and wrinkle her pointy nose, she wondered if today was going to be any different after all. Miss Forrester suddenly interrupted her pleasant flowing words and announced, "Children, we have a visitor today. May I introduce Mr. Luke Wheeler?"

Claire started in her seat and quickly turned to the door. There he was all right, good old Luke, standing about ten feet tall as it appeared to Claire. He filled the doorway with his head bent and smiled kindly at the children. "Do come in, Mr. Wheeler."

As Luke entered the room and made his way to the front of the class, the children tittered and chattered. "Class, please. May we have your attention?" continued Miss Forrester, and the class obediently responded.

Miss Forrester pulled her chair around to face the classroom and placed another large chair beside hers before Luke knew what was happening. He blushed that he had not helped her. Then she said, "Please, sit down, Mr. Wheeler," and he obligingly sat.

She introduced him and explained, "Mr. Wheeler is going to start an adventure — something that you may wish to do when you are old enough. I will ask Mr. Wheeler some questions, and he will share his plans. Then later, we will let you ask the questions. Now, Mr. Wheeler, what occupation have you selected?"

"I have chosen to be a preacher."

"And why have you decided this?"

"Well, my father is a preacher, as most of you know, and when I was a lad, I wanted with all my heart to do what my father did. I watched him preach, and then I practiced on my brother, Ben. Later, when I was about twelve, I knew I had a real calling from God."

"A calling, can you explain this further to the class?" asked Miss Forrester.

"I'll try, but it's really something you cannot see or hear directly. Rather you sense it within yourself. It's a feeling, and you know what to do. Other people often point out your gifts; that is called confirmation."

"I see. And what exactly do you have to do to become a preacher?"

"I went to school like these children are doing until I graduated from the classroom. Then I went to a secondary school. Now I need to go to a university to continue with more studying."

"And where will you go?"

"Ohio University in Athens, Ohio. If I need further schooling, I will go to the University of Pennsylvania," Luke answered proudly.

"Now, children, you may ask Mr. Wheeler questions."

Sammy raised his hand, and Miss Forrester promptly called upon him.

"W–will y–you p–preach here i–instead o–of your p–pa?"

"That is something I don't know yet. I'll have to wait and see where a preacher is needed when the time comes."

"H–how w–will you k–know where y–you're n–needed?" Sammy asked.

"People will write letters to me, asking me to come and be their preacher. Then I will pray about it."

Mary raised her hand shyly. "Yes, Mary?"

"How did you get so tall? Do all preachers have ta be tall?"

Luke answered quickly with a perfectly serious face, "I got to be so tall from eating all the food my mother put on my plate and from doing my chores without complaining. And God will take anyone, any size."

Claire smiled at that remark, knowing that Luke was teasing, but also happy that God would take her, just as she was.

Soon they exhausted the subject, and Miss Forrester dismissed the children to go home for the day. She thanked Luke warmly. "Whatever can I do to show you my appreciation?" she asked patting her little brown bun to coax her hairdo into place.

"It was my pleasure. You handle the children well. I must compliment you on your efforts."

Claire waited outside the classroom, wondering if they would ever finish talking when she heard the squeaking of the schoolroom floor.

"Luke!" she exclaimed.

"Hello, Claire."

"May I talk with you?"

"Of course. Would you like a ride?"

"Yes. Thank you."

He lifted her into the wagon with his strong arms and set her softly on the seat. "Now, what would you like to talk about?"

"Ministry. Are there women preachers?"

"Very few, but that does not mean women aren't important in ministry. There are many places women can serve."

"There are? Where?" she asked.

"Well, there are missions where women can work. Ladies go overseas as missionaries. Women marry preachers and support their husbands' work in the church. Women join groups or committees to help the needy and sick . . . or they can be nurses." He stopped there and looked over to see her response to this lengthy explanation.

"All that? How would I ever know where to start?"

Luke pulled the team to a stop and smiled tenderly at the girl beside him. "Is this something you want to do, Claire?"

"Oh, yes! I promised God I would. When Annabelle was sick, I told God that if He would heal her, I would go into ministry." She smiled proudly at her little speech.

"Well, God doesn't heal people because of promises they make, you know. He heals them just because He loves them, and He wants to."

"He does?" She looked disappointed. "Well, what would God think of me if I lied and didn't do what I promised?"

"I don't think He would consider that a lie. He can see right into our hearts. He would know that it was your love for Annabelle that was in your heart, and you didn't intend to lie."

"Well, maybe, but I will still go into ministry, just to be sure. So where should I start?"

"By reading your Bible. Read it every day if possible. Start praying. Just do whatever you would normally do, your everyday living. Then when God calls you into ministry, you will hear His voice. It will be a still, quiet voice inside you. Perhaps you will hear it from someone else. Things will fall into place automatically. You have to wait for Him to lead you."

"Can I come to you when I have questions? You're the most intelligent person I know."

"Of course. In fact, I'll give you my address so you can write to me while I'm at the university! How would you like that?"

"I'd rather have you here, but that would be nice. Thank you, Luke."

He gave her hand a loving squeeze, and they rode on. ⌐

CHAPTER 30

Mary Wheeler bustled about her warm, fragrant kitchen, preparing the turkey and stuffing for their Thanksgiving meal. They had invited the Tucker household as well as Buck and Thaddeas. Of course, the ladies at Tucker House would be bringing some of the food. Kate was famous for her pumpkin pies made from the plump ones grown in Mattie's garden patch. Mattie was bringing potatoes and pudding.

There was much to be done, and here she was with a household of men wanting to be of help but only getting in the way. The Reverend finally convinced her that he could wash dishes and clean the pots. Ben swept the sitting room and porch again so he could keep an eye out for the company. Luke took the boys to help with the chores.

The turkey smelled so tempting that the Reverend was hard put to keep his hands out of the roasting kettle in the stone oven.

"I hear a wagon. Must be the ladies from Tucker House already," Mary said, wiping her hands on her apron and patting her hair back. "Ben, would you greet them . . . ? Well, look at that, he's already half down the lane before I even get the words out," she exclaimed to her husband.

"Can't say as I blame him, Mary. He doesn't see Kate as often as I saw you before we were married, and that wasn't enough."

Soon the house was invaded by giggling, chattering women along with Thaddeas and the sheriff. "Why, I don't recognize this place, you got it lookin' so homey, Mary. Oh, no harm intended, Reverend," Mattie exclaimed.

"None taken. I agree; Mary is just what we needed around here."

"I think I'll steal Kate for awhile, Mary, unless you need her," Ben said.

"Of course, off with you," she answered.

Meanwhile, Annabelle looked around thinking that it did seem familiar. She went to chat with James and Frank, having remembered meeting them a few weeks earlier at church.

The Reverend announced, "Dinner is ready. We'll pray, and then all file past the food. Just fill your plates and find a seat wherever you can."

After the prayer, Ben and Luke told the story of their hunting escapade — the prize being the day's main course. Luke had tripped and fallen into a mud hole, allowing Ben to shoot the bird. Upon Luke's return to the farm, he had been humiliated when James and Frank had giggled at his muddied trousers. It was not quite the image he wanted to portray.

After dinner, the men retired to the sitting room. The young men challenged each other to checkers and a marble game that the Potter boys' pa had made. Mary, Mattie, and the girls saw to clearing and cleaning the dinner table. "Sounds rowdy in there for checkers," Kate exclaimed, sneaking a peak into the sitting room.

"Aw, you ain't heard nothin' yet," Mary said. The ladies laughed at the joke.

The afternoon flew by as Kate let her thoughts run wild. She imagined herself sitting by the fire with Ben, or pouring his coffee for him in the big chair with his feet propped up on the foot stool.

All too soon the sheriff commented, "Look at those dark clouds. A storm's a-brewing for sure!" A look out the window convinced the others, and they scurried to collect their belongings and put on their coats. Quickly and thoroughly, they thanked their hosts and made their way to the wagon.

Ben helped Kate into the wagon. The sheriff and Mattie climbed into the front while Thaddeas and the girls settled themselves in the back. They covered themselves with blankets to prepare for the cold ride home. Ben gave Kate's hand a squeeze and whispered, "I'm sorry we didn't get much time alone. I'll be over Saturday night, if I may?"

"Of course. I'll count the minutes."

Kate waved gaily as the wagon rolled out the lane.

Annabelle commented, "They are very nice people."

Whenever Annabelle said something to remind the others that she was still at a loss for remembering, it dampened their spirits.

"Annabelle?" Kate said on impulse.

"Yes?"

"See if you can remember anything about that night, the night of your birthday party."

"Kate!" Thaddeas interrupted. "Please!"

"No, it's all right," Annabelle said sadly. "I need to do this. What should I remember, Kate?"

"Well, you were in the back of a wagon like this with your friends. There was hay in the wagon, and you were singing songs.

Thaddeas was up front, driving the wagon."

"Thaddeas?" Annabelle interrupted. "Thaddeas?"

"Y–yes. It was I, Annabelle. I'm so sorry; I ran over you and . . ."

"It wasn't your fault at all. Don't go feeling sorry for me. I won't have it. Go on, Kate."

"Sammy Hawkes had just been dropped off."

"Sammy Hawkes?" she asked.

"Yes, you know, Claire's friend who stutters."

"Kate! What a cruel thing to say about my friend!" Claire piped up.

"Sorry, Claire. I didn't mean it that way."

Claire settled back into her corner, pulling her blanket tightly around her, unsure whether to defend him further, when Kate continued.

"He left his hat, and you saw it and stood up to get his attention when the wagon jolted, and you fell out."

Annabelle concentrated very hard on this scenario, willing herself to remember. Finally, she shook her auburn head sadly. "I'm sorry. I just can't remember."

Just then a loud cracking sound turned everyone's attention to the weather overhead. "Oh, no, we're in for it now," Thaddeas warned. "Cover up with your blankets as best you can. I don't think we're gonna make it home before it starts."

"Cuddle together," Claire said innocently.

"Come on, don't be bashful," Thaddeas said, following Claire's suggestion. He was sitting between Claire and Annabelle, and they giggled as they moved in closer.

The rain pelted as if venting out anger for a wrong deed done.

"Ooh, this is fun," squealed Claire in delight.

"It's so cold," Kate screamed back.

"Move in closer," Thaddeas suggested.

"This is just like the day of the barn raising," yelled Annabelle.

"Yes, I remember. We all got soaked," said Claire.

"And you pouted about the Indians, Kate," Annabelle added.

"Annabelle!" They all screamed at once.

"You remembered!" Claire clapped her hands in delight.

"Yes! I remember clearly!" Annabelle exclaimed in joy.

Thus, Annabelle's memory returned in torrents fitting of the situation. The others continued to drill her and pull remnants of memory out of the deep, dark closets of her mind. It was a ride they would never forget.

The rain was falling mercilessly, but it did not matter for they were wet with happy tears.

When they reached Tucker House, Thaddeas hugged Annabelle tightly, exclaiming over and over again how happy he was for her. He sorely wished he could go inside and share in the happy event, but he knew they had to hurry off and get their horses out of the storm.

Mattie made a huge fire in the fireplace, and sitting in their nightclothes, the ladies stayed up until the wee hours of the morning listening to Annabelle's remembering.

CHAPTER 31

Mattie walked into Beaver Creek to inquire about a catalog order from Cooper's General Store. The air outside was biting cold, and she pulled her winter cloak tightly about her, though she was warmed from the inside out, thinking about the surprises she had planned.

"Well, look who the wind blew in!" Mr. Cooper said with a laugh. The old joke was fittingly appropriate.

"Indeed!" Mattie laughed. "And, I've come to inquire about some special things I ordered, if you recall, for Christmas?"

"Ah, yes. But I'm sorry, Mattie, they are not in yet, but any day now, any day!"

"Well, just be sure ya don't say anything if one of the girls comes in for somethin'," she warned.

"Oh, I'll remember for sure, Mattie," he assured her.

"Miss Tucker, hello. How is Annabelle?"

Dorie inquired cheerfully.

"Very fine. She's good as ever, and we're all so proud of her. We're thankful she's back to her normal self."

"I'm glad. I wish she could come for a visit. Could she, please?" Dorie pleaded.

"Of course, that's kind of ya to invite her, Dorie," said Mattie.

"How about Thursday then?"

"Thursday would be jest fine, and Annabelle will be excited that ya asked her."

"Thank you, Miss Tucker. I can't wait!"

"Good day to ya then, Mr. Cooper," Mattie said as she left. She was pleasantly surprised when she walked outdoors for snow, huge white flakes, fell, softly wetting her face and sticking to the ground. *Well I'll be!* she thought. *Our first snowfall. I always forget jest how lovely it is!* She felt as young as a schoolgirl as she went about the rest of her errands. Then she heard a call.

"Mattie!" The sheriff stuck his head out of his office. "Come here and visit for a spell!"

"All right, for a minute!" she called.

"Come in out of the snow. Why, you're getting all wet," he said, concerned.

"Isn't it jest beautiful?" she asked, brushing off her cloak and removing her bonnet while he held the door open for her.

"The first snowfall always is," he agreed, nodding his head. "Here, come sit by the fire." He motioned toward his cozy, warm sitting area by the big stone fireplace.

Mattie quickly obeyed. She visited the sheriff often when she came to town. His office was very masculinely trimmed with a set of deer antlers above the fireplace. On the mantel lay an old holster without pistols, fondly placed there when the sheriff received his new one. Also there were a few books for entertainment on long, lonely nights, and an old piece of wood he had been whittling. Directly in front of her on the rough wooden floor sprawled a huge black bearskin, enough to frighten any lady if she was not already used to it being there.

"Are you still cold?" he asked. "I'll get you a cup of coffee."

"I'm startin' ta thaw, but that sounds mighty temptin'."

The sheriff poured the piping hot coffee into two tin mugs and went back to sit beside her. "You sure look cheery enough. Is it 'cause Christmas is a-coming?" he asked.

"Yes, I think that's it. Of course, I have a lot of other reasons to be happy, ya know."

"Tell me, Mattie, what makes you so happy?"

"I'm happy that Annabelle is well again. She's excited about the season, and Dorie Cooper just invited her to come and spend Thursday with her. She'll be in fine tune when she hears that!"

"Yes, I suspect she will at that." He chuckled as he envisioned the two girls together. "And?"

"And I'm happy I'm my old self. I was a bit of a crab there for awhile, and I must apologize right now while I'm thinkin' on it. You were so helpful and supportive through that whole time, and I was jest terrible to ya, Buck."

"Nonsense; don't even mention it, Mattie. You know I care about you dearly. It hurt me to see your pain. I hope we don't ever have to go through something like that again."

"I agree, but if times get hard again, at least next time I'll have the Lord."

"Yep, He sure makes a difference," the sheriff agreed. Then he glanced out the window and said, "You know, Mattie, if it keeps snowing, I may have to take you home myself or just keep you here for a spell." With that remark, he gave her a wink.

"Oh, now, you get that right out of your

head, Buck," she teased.

Easily encouraged, he cautiously continued, "You look absolutely radiant today with your rosy cheeks." Mattie blushed profusely. "Have I told you before that I think you're a very beautiful and charming woman?"

"Yes, ya certainly have, and I thank ya again," she said warmly.

"I know we talked about this before, but I feel the need to bring it up again."

"Oh, please don't, Buck!"

"Mattie, I must. You know how I love you."

"I love ya, too, Buck," she said earnestly.

"Then what's holding you back from marrying me? Is it my job? If I quit sheriffing and get a respectable occupation, would you marry me then?"

"Oh, Buck, never!"

"Never?" he echoed sadly.

"Never would I want you ta change like that. Why, sheriffin' is what ya do, and you do it very well, and if I couldn't take ya like you are . . . then I wouldn't be a fittin' wife."

"Mattie, are you saying that you'll marry me?" he asked pleadingly.

"No, that's not what I'm tryin' to say. It's not anything on your part that's hinderin', but somethin' to do with myself."

"What? Why won't you tell me? I love you, Mattie."

She reached over and took his hand, "Buck, I'm sorry. I guess maybe I'm jest afraid of all the changes."

"We'd only make the ones you wanted to make."

"Please give me more time ta think this through. I know we can't go on this way. But, please, let me think about this a spell longer."

He placed her hands between both of his and said, "All right, a little longer, just a little longer."

"Now, I must be goin' if I'm ever to make it home," she said determinedly.

He released her hands and said sadly, "If you must. Are you sure you can make it home?"

She laughed. "Oh, I'm sure, ya old worry wart!" The sheriff helped Mattie into her cloak and watched her leave. Suddenly, he felt very lonely.

What is wrong with me? she thought as she plodded toward home. *How can I lead him on this way? I love him, but I'd have ta tell him about my past. I wonder if he's guessed by now why I always put him off? It would serve me right if he'd up and marry someone else. I'd deserve it.* She kicked the ground soundly, puffing as she walked homeward.

Abruptly she stopped in her tracks, whirled, and headed straight back to the sheriff's office. Moments later, she rapped on his heavy door.

"Mattie! What's wrong? Come in!" the sheriff exclaimed with concern.

"I–I jest came back to say yes, I'll marry ya," she blurted out.

"Mattie, oh, Mattie." The sheriff enveloped her in his arms.

"First, before we make any plans, I've got a story to tell ya. Buck, please sit down and listen."

CHAPTER 32

Christmas Eve arrived, and a new-fallen snow, fresh and pure, robed the townsfolk in a garment of peace. Was it any wonder that Mattie overflowed with goodwill and charity as she reflected on the miracle of Christmas?

"Oh, Kate, ya look beautiful!" Mattie exclaimed as Kate came down the stairs. Kate had paused for just a moment to gaze in astonishment at a bit of mistletoe that mysteriously appeared at the bottom of the steps before she replied.

"Thank you, Mattie. You look grand yourself. May I inquire as to the origin of this bit of greenery?"

"I confess, I did it. I thought there might be a few handsome gentlemen droppin' in tonight."

"Mattie! I can't believe you're owning up to it. You must be under a spell for sure!"

"I guess I am since I agreed to marry

Buck, and I think I'm as eager for Christmas as the girls," Mattie confessed. "Speakin' of the girls, I'd better go hurry them along. Our company could be here any moment."

Left alone, Kate looked about her, and everything looked just right. The smells of the greenery they had used to decorate, fresh coffee, cider, and pumpkin pie mingled sweetly. She felt beautiful tonight with her new soft-flowing green gown and her ebony hair trimmed in green ribbons.

She walked to the window and tried to peer out, but it was too dark to see. As she cupped her face in her hands, the warmth from her breath steamed up the cold window. *It's no use,* she thought, but then she heard bells. *I wonder? That must be Ben and Luke.* She raced to the door.

"A cutter! How wonderful!" she exclaimed as she welcomed them in.

"Yes, would you and the girls like to go for a ride?" Ben asked gaily.

"That will be delightful! Move in here close to the fire and warm up. Mattie and the girls should be down shortly. Here they come now."

Mattie descended just in time to answer the door herself as Buck and Thaddeas arrived. They had walked the short distance and took a moment to shake off the snow and stomp their feet before entering.

"Why, Miss Mattie, you look lovely," Thaddeas said as he walked past.

"A vision of loveliness, my dear," the sheriff added in a low voice and then held out his arm to escort her to the sitting room.

They all stood around the fire chatting for a moment, and then it was agreed that they would all go for a ride except Mattie and the sheriff. As they climbed into the cutter, Claire's blue eyes were on Luke. He felt her gaze and winked. She smiled broadly and continued to watch him, her hero.

This was just the moment he had hoped for. He squirmed and made a funny face.

"What's a-matter, Luke?"

"Come see."

She looked at him suspiciously. "What do you have in there?" She leaned closer.

"It is a Christmas surprise for you, Claire. Something to remember me by when I'm gone." Luke pulled a tiny fur ball from under his coat.

"Mew, mew," it said.

"A kitten! For me? Look, Kate, Annabelle!" She held the little kitten in the air, showing everyone.

Claire thanked Luke with a cold, wet peck on his cheek. "I shall name him Freckles 'cause he has freckles on his nose just like you!"

"I'm honored, Claire."

In the back of the cutter, Thaddeas asked Annabelle how her day with Dorie went.

"It was so fun!" she exclaimed. "It was exciting to watch people come to the store and pick up their Christmas orders, and we helped Mrs. Cooper make tarts and cookies. I think I'd enjoy living in town like you do, Thaddeas."

"Really?"

"Yes, it's so exciting with all the hustle and bustle."

"I'm glad you're back to your cheery self, Annabelle," Thaddeas said earnestly. "Are you warm enough?"

"Yes, I'm fine."

When they reached Tucker House again, Claire was the first to slide off the cutter. "Let's go to the kitchen and get him some milk," she said, toting Freckles.

"Go ahead. Kate and I will unhitch the horses," Ben offered.

Annabelle tagged after Claire, begging to hold the fur ball, and Luke and Thaddeas were amused by all the fuss. "Here, you hold her, Annabelle, while I pour her some milk," ordered Claire.

"Let me get that," Luke said, reaching for

the dish that Claire was trying to get in vain.

"I'll bet it comes in handy to be so tall," she said all in one breath. "Now put her down and see if she goes for it, Annabelle."

Out in the sitting room, Mattie and Buck talked in low tones at one end of the room when the small group clamored in upon them. Annabelle and Claire sat on the floor in front of the fire, playing with Freckles, while Luke and Thaddeas pulled up their chairs close by.

There was a short silence, and Thaddeas took advantage of it. "I have news!" he announced, beaming with pleasure. "I've found a job so I guess I'll be staying in Beaver Creek now for sure."

"Wonderful!" said Luke. "Tell us what it is."

"I'm the new accountant at Green's Mill. It isn't exactly what I want to do with my life, but it's a start in business anyway."

"I'm so glad for you," Mattie said.

"Me, too. I've gotten quite attached to this nephew of mine," the sheriff said fondly.

Meanwhile out in the barn, Ben was just finishing. Kate held the lantern, stomping one foot and then the other, trying to keep warm while he worked. "Are you cold?" he asked, taking the lantern from her and hanging it on a nearby post.

She looked lovingly into his blue eyes. She noticed his freckles — placed in just the right spots on his handsome face. Ben moved closer. Her face was only inches away, breathtakingly close — almost against his — and her soft brown eyes were so close he could see the green specks in them. He saw her black-velvet eyelashes, long and soft. In a moment, he leaned closer and pressed his lips on her sweet, soft ones.

Kate felt the gentleness of his kiss, not forceful like Tanner's. It drew her, and she reveled in the ecstasy of the moment. This was the kiss she had dreamed of; it was everything she had anticipated.

As Ben slowly drew back, he realized how vulnerable Kate was. He saw the flush to her face and the love in her eyes. He felt encouraged and said breathlessly, "My intentions are proper, I assure you, Kate. I love you. Will you marry me?"

"I'd be proud to be your wife, Ben."

"Sweetheart, you don't know how happy you've made me. This is all I could think of since we broke that chair that afternoon you decided to sit on my lap."

She giggled. "Ben! How ungentlemanly of you to bring that up just now."

Ben grinned. "Like I said, it's all I've been thinking about." Then he grew serious again. "There's something else that's been on my mind. I have a confession, and a question to ask you."

"You do? Whatever is it?"

"Well, I'm afraid I was eavesdropping one day, but I didn't mean to and didn't know you were there until I was right upon you. I thought you were crying because you had your head down and wondered what was wrong. Then I heard you praying. So I started to turn away, but I heard what you said. It was the time Annabelle got covered with bees."

"What did I say?"

"You told God about someone you'd met; you said he was handsome and strong and how much you were attracted to him. I guess I don't have the right to ask who it was, do I?"

"Of course you do. If we're to be married, we shouldn't be keeping any secrets from each other, should we?" Ben looked at her wondering if he really wanted to hear and whatever had possessed him to bring it up now. He waited patiently for her to go on. "It was you I was talking about, Silly. Don't you realize that you're the only man I've ever felt this way about?"

"I am? All this time I thought there was someone else."

"I thought you were mighty slow," she teased.

"Hey, now! Well, I guess I was, but not anymore." He placed his hands on her shoulders. "I'll do my best to make you happy, Kate, but I don't have any big plans like Luke. I'm just a simple man."

"You don't have to, Ben. Helping other people comes natural with you, and ministry follows you wherever you go."

"Why, Kate, you're trembling," he said. "Darling?"

She raised a shaking hand and touched his cheek. "With joy. I love you."

Ben pulled her close and held her tight for a moment, then he kissed her properly until her trembling ceased.

ABOUT THE AUTHOR

Dianne Christner and her husband make their home in Scottsdale, Arizona, enjoying the beauty of the desert. However, it is fond memories of her childhood spent in Ohio that inspired this book. After years of working as an executive secretary, she is happy to be able to spend her time at home writing or traveling and researching. If you enjoyed this book, she invites you to visit her website www.diannechristner.com so that you can meet her and her family members and follow her latest writing endeavors.

The employees of Thorndike Press hope you have enjoyed this Large Print book. All our Thorndike and Wheeler Large Print titles are designed for easy reading, and all our books are made to last. Other Thorndike Press Large Print books are available at your library, through selected bookstores, or directly from us.

For information about titles, please call:
(800) 223-1244

or visit our Web site at:
www.gale.com/thorndike
www.gale.com/wheeler

To share your comments, please write:
Publisher
Thorndike Press
295 Kennedy Memorial Drive
Waterville, ME 04901

CMK 4-23-08 ✓ R

R.

MAR 2 1 2008